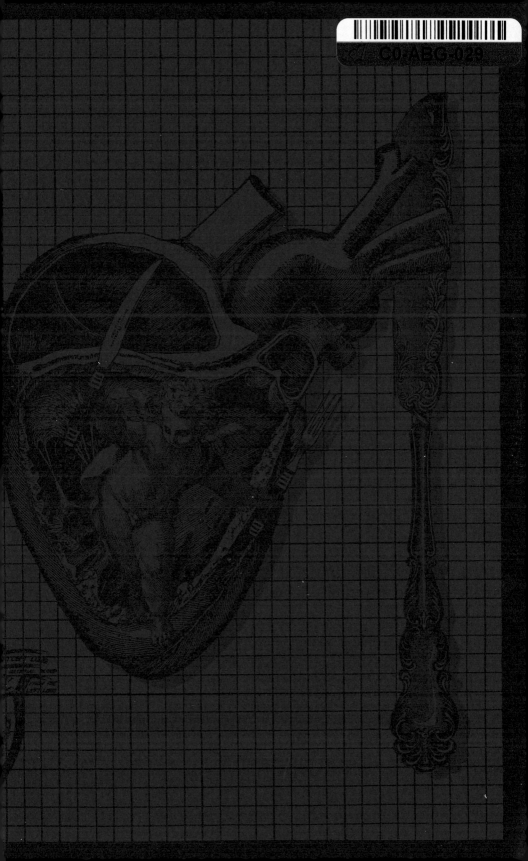

THE BRAINS OF RATS

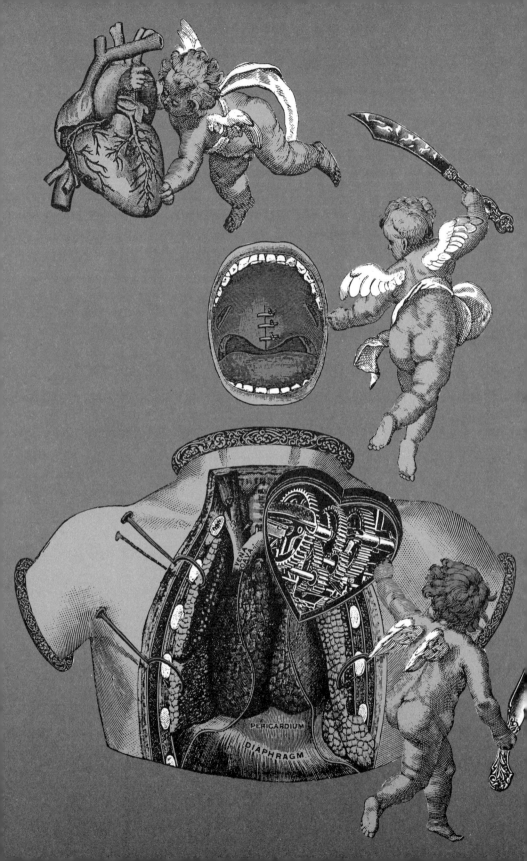

PERICARDIUM

DIAPHRAGM

MICHAEL BLUMLEIN

THE
BRAINS
OF
RATS

Illustrated by

T. M. CALDWELL

Introduction by

MICHAEL McDOWELL

SCREAM / PRESS

LOS ANGELES / 1990

MICHAEL BLUMLEIN

LOS CEREBROS DE RATAS

ACKNOWLEDGMENTS

The following stories have been previously published as noted:

"The Brains of Rats": *Interzone* #16, Summer 1986.
"Tissue Ablation...": *Interzone* #7, Spring 1984.
"The Domino Master": *Omni*, June 1988.
"Drown Yourself": *Mississippi Review* 47/48 Vol. 16, Numbers 2 & 3, 1988.
"Interview with C.W.": *New Pathways* #10, March 1988.
"Shed His Grace": SEMIOTEXT(e) Vol. V, Iss. 2 (#14), Autonomedia, 1990.
"The Promise of Warmth": *Twilight Zone*, August 1988.
"The Thing Itself": FULL SPECTRUM, Bantam Spectra Books, Sept. 1988.
"Bestseller": *Fantasy & Science Fiction*, January 1990.

The following stories are first publications:

"The Glitter and the Glamour"
"Keeping House"
"The Wet Suit"

ILLUSTRATIONS

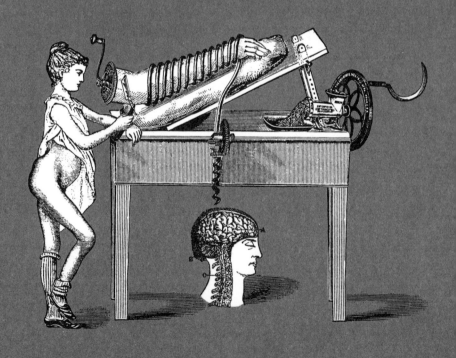

Introduction

by

Michael McDowell

A couple of years ago I was a judge for the World Fantasy Awards. I read yards of novels and feet of novellas and fathoms of short stories. Most bored or stifled me, some amount pleased me, a very very little excited me.

One thing knocked me out of the box.

It was a short story, appearing in *Interzone*, a British periodical I had never heard of. The story was called "The Brains of Rats".

I remember thinking: This man Blumlein is either mad or he's a better writer than I am. Neither his madness nor my jealousy could affect the splendor of the work, however, so I photocopied "The Brains of Rats" and sent it to the other judges, to make certain they wouldn't by any chance miss it. It was nominated for best short story.

I sent it to a great number of other people. The response was uniformly one of astonishment, bewilderment, and admiration.

I knew nothing of Michael Blumlein. I was reluctant to read anything else, dreading to find that "The Brains of Rats" was a fluke.

It was not. And other of his writings have astonished me more.

"Tissue Ablation", when I first read it, seemed to be about something else. That is, I could scarcely credit its grotesque and

politically-charged audacity. I short-changed the piece, which is
an Inquisitional anathema in the house style of the *New England
Journal of Medicine*. It is as savage as Swift's "A Modest Proposal",
and every bit as angry.

Blumlein's is a dignity of narration delineating madness and
aberration. Even the stories that are "predictable" such as the
Who's-the-Android narrative of "Drown Yourself" become trea-
tises on passion and obsession. The futured world of Blumlein's
occasional science fiction stories is strange and unsettling.
Fellini's stylized and grotesque cinematic past is probably nearest
it, not because its details are correct but simply because history is
shown to be alien and unrecognizable. For we are not what we
were. We do not recognize ourselves in Blumlein's future, for the
same reason — we are not what we will become.

Michael Blumlein has a medical background, and currently
practices medicine. For me to write anymore of his past, or present, or private life — even if I knew it to reveal — would seem to
me to be an attempt to explain (or explain away) some of the
more obvious slants of his writing.

The fact is, I don't know of any other writer who has so
deeply mined his most obvious identity (as a doctor who both
practices and teaches medicine) to such great and transcendent
effect. There are legions of writers whose protagonists happen to
be writers as well, and movie stars turn out paperback originals
about the movie industry. Other doctors-turned-novelists have
employed medical venues to elevate their heavily choreographed
plots and make them seem more exotic. But Blumlein writes of
healers and healing the way Eudora Welty writes about the South.
Medicine is his palette not his picture. Blumlein's subjects are
gender, madness, deformity, and other infirmities of the soul.

Blumlein's scientific and medical background serve to reinforce our belief in his narrations. In "The Brains of Rats", in other
stories, in a forthcoming novel I've been privileged to read, the

narrator's textbook descriptions of nature's pathology — aberrations sanctioned in fiction only by their reality — segue (or rather dog-leg) abruptly into the pathology of the civilized mind. What Blumlein smears on the glass slide is a cross-section of irreality. The more "scientific"' or "clinical" the story —"Tissue Ablation" the most obvious case in point — the more that story operates by an internal rhythm not of intellect but of emotion. The cold intern melts to reveal the shimmering hot shaman in his heart:

> Love requires health. Health is hypnotism, trust, science. It is persuasion and power, belief spread like a blanket, a bed. It is rational, irrational. Chemistry, words, light and sound.

Here, as elsewhere in Blumlein, incantation becomes illumination.

Blumlein's technique is superb. By which I mean that word upon word and sentence upon sentence and paragraph upon paragraph Blumlein's narrative accomplishes precisely what he wants it to accomplish. As a fellow craftsman I praise and envy his brave reliance on the rhythmic engineering of unadorned nouns and verbs. With authority that is both clinical and mythic, Blumlein declaims:

> An agent can be employed. A drug, for example, a root. Or a shell, mud, bark, the husk of an insect. A scalpel can be the agent. The ace of cups. There are capsules the size of cherries, poultices that smell like tar. Horn of goat, spore of fungus, fender, headlight, bottle-cap. A healer must not be narrow-minded.

Blumlein's prose has the skeletal grace of an engraving in *Gray's Anatomy*.

When I first read "The Brains of Rats", I was astonished by the voice of the male narrator — I had never heard a man speak with such considered self-deprecation of his sexuality, or exhibit so much thoughtful but relentless vulnerability. Even more startling was the quiet sadness with which Blumlein's narrator set forth his unpopular and very politically incorrect position on the final inequality of the sexes (and I do not speak socially or morally here but rather psychically). In all of his work, Blumlein writes of men and women as if they were two different species, with scant hope of final congruence or emotional reciprocity.

Blumlein's characters are the strangers whose faces we know from parking lots and elevators, whose paychecks bear the same stamped comptroller's signature as ours, but whose real lives are as distant and unimaginable as Tamburlaine's. They are the mad and violent, and the obsessive.

I have always wanted for someone to write of *real* fetishism — sexual obsessions are not all stilettos and whips and Oriental Housewives in Cellophane. A real fetish is as mundane as the table, or bed, or toilet eccentricities of your next-door neighbor, your parents, your significant other. How many American men harden for long blonde hair; how many American women dampen before a shop window filled with heeled shoes? How "The Wet Suit" ends — without resolution, or confrontation, or escalation — is its real and stunning point and purpose.

All in all, Blumlein writes of the rational man (be he the central character or — more often — the narrator) who tells his story in self-absorption, while we hear another but parallel tale of irrationality. In all the stories — even the ones that most perplex me — there's an internal, emotional, satisfying surge of rhythm, a sure precision of the narrator's idiosyncratic diction, and an unpredictable unfolding of events. And each story has an odd, inevitable, disturbing finality — a thing quite distinct for a mere ending.

Blumlein, time after time, acknowledges and delineates the madness of genes and species and gender. He concludes, with the razor's truth, that mapping and exegesis are insufficient for understanding, much less for healing.

It is as if we had stumbled into an anatomy class when we

had been searching for the hospital gift shop, to find Michael Blumlein standing beside a specimen of recently departed humanity. The scalpel flashes and the tiny circular saw spins and hums. In glaring light we see, intricate and improbable, what we are beneath our skin.

MICHAEL MCDOWELL
20 July 1989

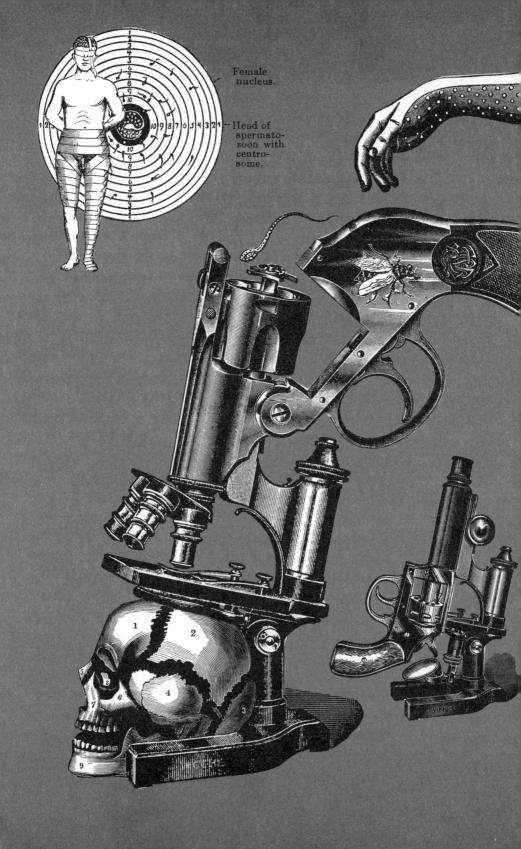

Female
nucleus.

Head of
spermato-
zoön with
centro-
some.

THE BRAINS OF RATS

There is evidence that Joan of Arc was a man. Accounts of her trial state that she did not suffer the infirmity of women. When examined by the prelates prior to her incarceration it was found that she lacked the characteristic escutcheon of women. Her pubic area, in fact, was as smooth and hairless as a child's.[1]

There is a condition of men, of males, called testicular feminization. The infants are born without a penis, and the testicles are hidden. The external genitalia are those of a female. Raised as women, these men at puberty develop breasts. Their voices do not deepen. They do not menstruate because they lack a uterus. They have no pubic hair.

These people carry a normal complement of chromosomes. The twenty-third pair, the so-called sex chromosome pair, is unmistakably male. XY. Declared a witch in 1431 and burned at the stake at the age of nineteen, Joan of Arc was quite likely one of these.

Herculine Barbin was born in 1838 in France; she was reared as a female. She spent her childhood in a convent and in boarding schools for girls and later became a schoolmistress. Despite her rearing, she had the sexual inclination of a male. She had already taken a female lover, when, on account of severe pain in her left groin, she sought the advice of a physician. Partly as a

1

result of his examination her sex was redesignated, and in 1860 she was given the civil status of a male. The transformation brought shame and disgrace upon her. Her existence as a male was wretched, and in 1868 she took her own life.[2]

I have a daughter. I am married to a blond-haired, muscular woman. We live in enlightened times. But daily I wonder who is who and what is what. I am baffled by our choices; my mind is unclear. Especially now that I have the means to ensure that every child born on this earth is male.

A patient once came to me, a man with a painful drip from the end of his penis. He had had it for several days; neither excessive bathing nor drugstore remedies had proven helpful. About a week and a half before, on a business trip, he had spent time with a prostitute. I asked if he had enjoyed himself. In a roundabout way he said it was natural for a man.

Several days later, at home, his daughter tucked safely in bed, he had made love to his wife. He said that she got very excited. The way he said it made me think she was the only one in the room.

The two of them are both rather young. While he was in the examining room, she sat quietly in the waiting room. She stared ahead, fatigue and ignorance making her face impassive. In her lap her daughter was curled asleep.

In the room the man milked his penis, squeezing out a large amount of creamy material, which I smeared on a glass slide. In an hour the laboratory told me he had gonorrhea. When I conveyed the news to him, he was surprised and worried.

"What is that?" he asked.

"An infection," I said. "A venereal disease. It's spread through sexual contact."

He nodded slowly. "My wife, she got too excited."

"Most likely you got it from the prostitute."

He looked at me blankly and said it again. "She got too excited."

I was fascinated that he could hold such a notion and calmly repeated what I had said. I recommended treatment for both him and his wife. How he would explain the situation to her was up to him. A man with his beliefs would probably not have too hard a time.

I admit that I have conflicting thoughts. I am intrigued by hypnotism and the relations of power. For years I have wanted to be a woman, with small, firm breasts held even firmer by a brassiere. My hair would be shoulder-length and soft. It would pick up highlights and sweep down over one ear. The other side of my head would be bare, save for some wisps of hair at the nape and around my ear. I would have a smooth cheek.

I used to brush it this way, posing before my closet mirror in dark tights and high-heeled boots. The velveteen dress I wore was designed for a small person, and I split the seams the first time I pulled it over my head. My arms and shoulders are large; they were choked by the narrow sleeves. I could hardly move, the dress was so tight. But I was pretty. A very pretty thing.

I never dream of having men. I dream of women. I am a woman and I want women. I think of being simultaneously on the top and on the bottom. I want the power and I want it taken from me.

I should mention that I also have the means to make every conceptus a female. The thought is as disturbing as making them all male. But I think it shall have to be one or the other.

The genes that determine sex lie on the twenty-third pair of chromosomes. They are composed of a finite and relatively short sequence of nucleic acids on the X chromosome and one on the Y. For the most part these sequences have been mapped.

Comparisons have been made between species. The sex-determining gene is remarkably similar in animals as diverse as the wasp, the turtle and the cow. Recently it has been found that the male banded krait, a poisonous snake of India separated evolutionarily from man by many millions of years, has a genetic sequence nearly identical to that of the human male.

The Y gene turns on other genes. A molecule is produced, a complex protein, which is present on the surface of virtually all cells in the male. It is absent in the female. Its presence makes cells and environments of cells develop in particular ways. These ways have not changed much in millions of years.

Certain regions of the brain in rats show marked sexual specificity. Cell density, dendritic formation, synaptic configuration of the male are different from the female. When presented with two solutions of water, one pure, the other heavily sweetened with saccharin, the female rat consistently chooses the latter. The male does just the opposite. Female chimpanzee infants exposed to high levels of male hormones in utero exhibit patterns of play different from their sisters. They initiate more, are rougher and more threatening. They tend to snarl alot.

Sexual differences of the human brain exist, but they have been obscured by the profound evolution of this organ in the past half-million years. We have speech and foresight, consciousness and self-consciousness. We have art, physics and religion. In a language whose meaning men and women seem to share, we say we are different, but equal.

The struggles between sexes, the battles for power are a reflection of the schism between thought and function, between the power of our minds and powerlessness in the face of our design. Sexual equality, an idea present for hundreds of years, is subverted by instincts present for millions. The genes determining mental capacity have evolved rapidly; those determining sex have been stable for eons. Humankind suffers the consequences of this disparity, the ambiguities of identity, the violence between the sexes. This can be changed. It can be ended. I have the means to do it.

All my life I have watched men fight with women. Women with men. Women come to the clinic with bruised and swollen cheeks, where they have been slapped and beaten by their lovers. Not long ago an attractive middle-aged lady came in with a bloody nose, bruises on her arms and a cut beneath her eye, where the cheek bone rises up in a ridge. She was shaking uncontrollably, sobbing in spasms so that it was impossible to understand what she was saying. Her sister had to speak for her.

Her boss had beat her up. He had thrown her against the filing cabinets and kicked her on the floor. She had cried for him to stop, but he had kept on kicking. She had worked for him for ten years. Nothing like this had ever happened before.

Another time a young man came in. He wore a tank-top and had big muscles in his shoulders and arms. On one bicep was a tattoo of the upper torso and head of a woman, her huge breasts bursting out of a ragged garment. On his forearm beneath this picture were three long and deep tracks in the skin, oozing blood. I imagined the swipe of a large cat, a lynx or a mountain lion. He told me he had hurt himself working on his car.

I cleaned the scratches, cut off the dead pieces of skin bunched up at the end of the tracks. I asked again. It was his girlfriend, he said, smiling now a little, gazing proudly at the marks on his arm. They had had a fight, she had scratched him with her nails. He looked at me, turning more serious, trying to act like a man but sounding like a boy, and asked, you think I should have a shot for rabies?

Sexual differentiation in humans occurs at about the fifth week of gestation. Prior to this time the fetus is sexless, or more precisely, it has the potential to become either (or both) sex. Around the fifth week a single gene turns on, initiating a cascade of events that ultimately gives rise to testicle or ovary. In the male this gene is associated with the Y chromosome; in the female, with the X. An XY pair normally gives rise to a male; an XX pair, to a female.

The two genes have been identified and produced by artificial means. Despite a general reluctance in the scientific community as a whole, our laboratory has taken this research further. Recently, we have devised a method to attach either gene to a common rhinovirus. The virus is ubiquitous; among humans it is highly contagious. It spreads primarily through water droplets (sneezing, coughing), but also through other bodily fluids (sweat, urine, saliva, semen). We have attenuated the virus so that it is harmless to mammalian tissue. It incites little, if any, immune response, resting dormantly inside cells. It causes no apparent disruption of function.

When an infected female becomes pregnant, the virus rapidly crossed the placenta, infecting cells of the developing fetus. If the virus carried the X gene, the fetus will become a female; if it carries the Y, a male. In mice and rabbits we have been able to produce entire litters of male or female. Experiments in simians have been similarly successful. It is not premature to conclude that we have the capability to do the same for humans.

Imagine whole families of male or female. Districts, towns, even countries. So simple, it is as though it was always meant to be.

My daughter is a beautiful girl. She knows enough about sex, I think, to satisfy her for the present. She plays with herself often at night, sometimes during the day. She is very happy not to have to wear diapers anymore. She used to look at my penis a lot, and once in a while she would touch it. Now she doesn't seem to care.

Once maybe every three or four months she'll put on a pair of pants. The rest of the time she wears skirts or dresses. My wife, a laborer, wears only pants. She drives a truck.

One of our daughter's school teachers, a Church woman, told her that Christian girls don't wear pants. I had a dream last night that our next child is a boy.

I admit I am confused. In the ninth century there was a German woman with a name no one remembers. Call her Katrin. She met and fell in love with a man, a scholar. Presumably, the love was mutual. The man travelled to Athens to study and Katrin went with him. She disguised herself as a man so that they could live together.

In Athens the man died. Katrin stayed on. She had learned much from him, had become something of a scholar herself. She continued her studies and over time gained renown for her learning. She kept her disguise as a man.

Sometime later she was called to Rome to study and teach at the offices of Pope Leo IV. Her reputation grew, and when Leo died in 855, Katrin was elected Pope.

Her reign ended abruptly two and a half years later. In the midst of a papal procession through the streets of Rome, her cloak hanging loose, obscuring the contours of her body, Katrin squatted on the ground, uttered a series of cries and delivered a baby. Soon after, she was thrown in a dungeon, and later banished to an impoverished land to the north. From that time on, all popes, prior to confirmation, have been examined by two reliable clerics. Before an assembled audience they feel under his robes.

"Testiculos habet," they declare, at which point the congregation heaves a sigh of relief.

"Deo gratias," it chants back. "Deo gratias." [3]

I was at a benefit luncheon the other day, a celebration of regional women writers. Of five hundred people I was one of a handful of men. I went at the invitation of a friend because I like the friend and I like the writers who were being honored. I wore a sports coat and slacks and had a neatly trimmed four day growth of beard. I waited in a long line at the door, surrounded by women. Some were taller than me, but I was taller than most. All were dressed fashionably; most wore jewelry and makeup. I was uncomfortable in the crowd, not profoundly, but enough that my manner turned meek. I was ready for a fight.

A loud woman butted in front of me and I said nothing. At the registration desk I spoke softly, demurely. The woman at the desk smiled and said something nice. I felt a little better, took my card and went in.

It was a large and fancy room, packed with tables draped with white cloths. The luncheon was being catered by a culinary school located in the same building. There was a kitchen on the ground floor, to the left of the large room. Another was at the mezzanine level above the stage at the front of the room. This one was enclosed in glass, and during the luncheon there was a class going on. Students in white coats and a chef with a tall white hat passed back and forth in front of the glass. Their lips moved, but from below we didn't hear any sounds.

Mid-way through the luncheon the program started. The main organizer spoke about the foundation for which the luncheon was a benefit. It is an organization dedicated to the empowerent of women, to the rights of women and girls. My mind drifted.

I have been a feminist for years. I was in the room next door when my first wife formed a coven. I told her it was good. I celebrated with her the publication of Valerie Solanas's *The S.C.U.M. Manifesto*. The sisters made a slide show, using some of Valerie's words. It was shown around the East Coast. I helped them out by providing a man's voice. I am a turd, the man said. A lowly, abject turd.

My daughter is four. She is a beautiful child. I want her to be able to choose. I want her to feel her power. I will tear down the door that is slammed in her face because she is a woman.

The first honoree came to the podium, reading a story about the bond between a wealthy woman traveler and a poor Mexican room-maid. After two paragraphs a noise interrupted her. It was a dull, beating sound, went on for half a minute, stopped, started up again. It came from the glassed-in teaching kitchen above the stage. The white-capped chef was pounding a piece of meat, oblivious to the scene below. Obviously he could not hear.

The woman tried to keep reading but could not. She made one or two frivolous comments to the audience. We were all a little nervous, and there were scattered titters while we waited for something to be done. The chef kept pounding the meat. Behind me a woman whispered loudly, male chauvinist.

I was not surprised, had, in fact, been waiting from the beginning for someone to say something like that. It made me mad. The man was innocent. The woman was a fool. A robot. I wanted to shake her, shake her up and make her pay.

I have a friend, a man with a narrow face and cheeks that always look unshaven. His eyes are quick; when he is with me, they always seem to be looking someplace else. He is facile with speech and quite particular about the words he chooses. He is not unattractive.

I like this man for the same reasons I dislike him. He is opportunistic and assertive. He is clever, in the way that being detached allows one to be. And fiercely competitive. He values those who rise to his challenges.

I think of him as a predator, as a man looking for an advantage. This would surprise, even bewilder him, for he carries the innocence of self-absorption. When he laughs at himself, he is so proud to be able to do so.

He has a peculiar attitude toward women. He does not like those who are his intellectual equal. He does not respect those who are not. And yet he loves women. He loves to make them. Especially he loves the ones who need to be convinced. I sometimes play tennis with him. I apologize if I hit a bad shot. I apologize if I am not adequate competition. I want to please him, and I lose every time we play. I am afraid to win, afraid that he might get angry, violent. He could explode.

I want to win. I want to win bad. I want to drive him into the net, into the concrete itself and beneath it with the force of my victory.

I admit I am perplexed. A man is aggressive, tender, strong, compassionate, hostile, moody, loyal, competent, funny, generous, searching, selfish, powerful, self-destructive, shy, shameful, hard, soft, duplicit, faithful, honest, bold, foolhardy, vain, vulnerable and proud. Struggling to keep his instincts in check, he is both abused and blessed by his maleness:

Dr. P, a biologist, husband and father never knew how much of his behavior to attribute to the involuntary release of chemicals, to the flow of electricity through synapses stamped male as early as sixty days after conception, and how much to reckon under his control. He did not want to dilute his potency as a scientist, as a man, by struggling too hard against his impulses, and yet the glimpses he had of another way of life were often too compelling to disregard. The bond between his wife and daughter sometimes brought tears to his eyes. The thought of his wife carrying the child in her belly for nine months and pushing her out through the tight gap between her legs sometimes settled in his mind like a hypnotic suggestion, like something so sweet and pure that he would wither without it.[4]

I asked another friend what it was to him to be a man. He laughed nervously and said the question was too hard. Okay, I said, what is it you like best? He shied away but I pressed him. Having a penis, he said. I nodded. Having it sucked, putting it in a warm place. Coming. He smiled and looked beatific. Oh God, he said, it's so good to come.

Later on he said, I like the authority I have, the subtle edge. I like the respect. A man, just by being a man, gets respect. When I get an erection, when I get very hard, I feel strong. I take on power that at other times is hidden. Impossibilities seem to melt away.

(A world like that, I think. A world of men. How wondrous! The Y virus then. I think it must be the Y.)

In the summer of our marriage I was sitting with my first wife in the mountains. She was on one side of a dirt road that wound up to a pass and I was on the other. Scattered on the mountain slope were big chunks of granite and around them stands of aspen and a few solitary pines. The sky was a deep blue, the kind that makes you suck in your breath. The air was crisp.

She was throwing rocks at me, and arguing. Some of the rocks were quite big, as big as you could hold in a palm. They landed close, throwing up clouds of dust in the roadbed. She was telling me why we should get married.

"I'll get more respect," she said. "Once we get married then we can get divorced. A divorced woman gets respect."

I asked her to stop throwing rocks. She was mad because she wasn't getting her way. Because I was being truculent. Because she was working a man's job cleaning out the insides of ships, scaling off the plaque and grime, and she was being treated like a woman. She wanted to be treated like a man, be tough like a man, dirty and tough. She wanted to smoke in bars, get drunk, shoot pool. In the bars she wanted to act like a man, be loud, not take shit. She wanted to do this and also she wanted to look sharp, she wanted to dress sexy, in tight blouses and pants. She wanted men to come on to her, she wanted them to fawn a little. She wanted the power.

"A woman who's been married once, they know she knows something. She's not innocent. She's gotten rid of one, she can get rid of another. They show a little respect."

She stopped throwing rocks and came over to me. I was a little cowed. She said that if I loved her I would marry her so she could divorce me. She was tender and insistent. I did love her, and I understood the importance of respect. But also I was mixed-up. I couldn't make up my mind.

"You see," she said, angry again, "you're the one who gets to decide. It's always you who's in control."

"I am a turd," I replied. "A lowly, abject turd."

A woman came to me the other day. She knew my name, was aware of the thrust of my research but not the particulars. She did not know that in the blink of an eye her kind, or mine, could be gone from the face of the earth. She did not know, but it did not seem to matter.

She was dressed simply; her face was plain. She seemed at ease when she spoke, though she could not conceal (nor did she try) a certain intensity of feeling. She said that as a woman she could not trust a man to make decisions regarding her future. To my surprise I told her that I am not a man at all.

"I am a mother," I said. "When my daughter was an infant, I let her suckle my breast."

"You have no breasts," she said scornfully.

"Only no milk." I unbuttoned my shirt and pulled it to the side. I squeezed a nipple. "She wouldn't stay on because it was dry."

"You are a man," she said, unaffected. "You look like one. I've seen you walk, you walk like one."

"How does a man walk?"

"Isn't it obvious?"

"I am courteous. I step aside in crowds, wait for others to pass."

"Courtesy is the manner the strong adopt toward the weak. It is the recognition of their dominance."

"Sometimes I am meek," I said. "Sometimes I'm quite shy."

She gave me an exasperated look, as though I were a child who had strained the limits of her patience. "You are a man, and men are outcasts. You are outcasts from the very world you made. The world you built on the bodies of other species. Of women."

I did not want to argue with her. In a way she was right. Men have tamed the world.

"You think you rise above," she went on, less stridently. "It is the folly of comparison. There's no one below. No one but yourselves."

"I don't look down," I said.

"Men don't look at all. If you did, you'd see that certain parts of your bodies are missing."

"What does that mean?"

She looked at me quietly. "Don't you think it's time women had a chance?"

"Let me tell you something," I said. "I have always wanted to be a woman. I used to dress like one whenever I had the chance. I was too frightened to keep women's clothes in my own apartment, and I used to borrow my neighbor's. She was a tall woman, bigger than me, and she worked evenings. I had the key to her apartment, and at night after work, before she came home, I would sneak into her place and go through her drawers. Because of her size, most of her clothes fit. She had a pair of boots, knee-high soft leather boots which I especially liked."

"Why are you telling me this?" she asked suspiciously.

"I want to. It's important that you understand."

"Listen, no man wants to be a woman. Not really. Not deep down."

"Men are beautiful." I made a fist. "Our bodies are powerful, like the ocean, and strong. Our muscles swell and tuck into each other like waves.

"There is nothing so pure as a man. Nothing like the face of a boy. The smooth and innocent cheek. The promise in the eyes.

"I love men. I love to trace our hard parts, our soft ones with my eyes, my imagination. I love to see us naked, but I am not aroused. I never have thoughts of having men.

"One night, though, I did. I was coming from my neighbor's apartment, where I had dressed up pretty in dark tights, those high boots of hers, and a short, belted dress. I had stuffed socks in the cups of her bra and was a very stacked lady. When I was done, I took everything off, folded it and put it neatly back in the drawers. I got dressed in my own pants and shirt, a leather jacket on top, and left. I was going to spend the night with my wife.

"On the street I still felt aroused. I had not relieved the tension and needed some release. As I walked, I alternated between feeling like a man on the prowl and a woman wanting to grab something between her legs. I think I felt more the latter, because I wanted something to be done to me. I wanted someone else to be boss.

"I started down the other side of the hill that separated my house from my wife's. It was late and the street was dark. A single car, a Cadillac, crept down the hill. When it came to me, it slowed. The driver motioned me over and I moved away. My heart skittered. He did it again and I swallowed and went to him.

"He was a burly black man, smelled of alcohol. I sat far away from him, against the door, and stared out the windshield. He asked where was my place. I said I had none. He grunted and drove up a steep hill and several more. He pulled the big car into the basement lot of an apartment complex. 'A ladyfriend's,' he said, and I followed him up some flights of stairs and down a corridor to the door of the apartment. I was aroused, frightened, determined. I don't think he touched me that whole time.

"He opened the door and we went in. The living room was bare, except for a record player on the floor and a scattered bunch of records. There was a record on, about two-thirds done, and I expected to see someone else in the apartment. But it was empty.

"The man went into another room, maybe the kitchen, and fixed himself a drink. He wasn't friendly to me, wasn't cruel. I think he was a little nervous to have me there, but otherwise acted as if I were a piece of something to deal with in his own way at his own time. I did not feel that I needed to be treated any differently than that.

"He took me into the bedroom, put me on the bed. That was in the beginning: later I remember only the floor. He took off his shirt and his pants and pulled my pants down. He settled on me, his front to my front. He was barrelchested, big and heavy. I wrapped my legs around him and he began to rub up and down on me. His lips were fat, and he kissed me hard and tongued me. He smelled very strong, full of drugs and liquor. His beard was rough on my cheek. I liked the way it felt but not the way it scratched. He began to talk to himself.

"'The swimmin' gates,' he muttered. 'Let me in the swimmin' gates. The swimmin' gates.'

"He said these words over and over, drunkenly, getting more and more turned on. He rolled me over, made me squat on my knees with my butt in the air. He grabbed me with his arms, tried to enter me. I was very dry and it hurt. I let him do it despite the pain because I wanted to feel it, I wanted to know what it was like. I didn't want to let him down.

"Even before then, before the pain, I had withdrawn. I was no longer aroused, or not much. I liked his being strong because I wanted to be dominated, but as he got more and more excited, I lost a sense that I was anything at all. I was a man, but I might just as easily have been a woman, or a dog, or even a tube lined with fur. I felt like nothing; I was out of my body and growing cold. I did not even feel the power of having brought him to his climax. If it wasn't me, it would have been something else . . ."

I stopped. The woman was quiet for awhile.

"So what's your point?" she asked.

"I'm wrong to think he didn't need me. Or someone, to do what he wanted. To take it without question."

"He hurt you."

"In a way I pity him. But also, I admire his determination."

She was upset. "So you think you know what it's like to be a woman? Because of that you think you know?"

"I don't know anything," I said. "Except that when I think about it I always seem to know more about what it is to be a woman than what it is to be a man."

Having a penis, my friend said. That's what I like best. It reminds me of a patient I once had, a middle-aged man with diabetes. He took insulin injections twice a day, was careful with his diet, and still he suffered the consequences of that disease. Most debilitating to him was the loss of his sex life.

"I can't get it up," he told me. "Not for more than a minute or two."

I asked if he came. Diabetes can be quite selective in which nerves it destroys.

"Sometimes. But it's not the same. It feels all right, it feels good, but it's not the same. A man should get hard."

I nodded, thinking that he should be grateful, it could be worse. "At least you can come. Some people can't even do that."

"Don't you have some shot, Doc? Something so I can get it up."

I said no, I didn't, it wasn't a question of some shot, it was a question of his diabetes. We agreed to work harder at keeping it under control, and we did, but his inability to get an erection remained. He didn't become depressed, as many do, nor did he get angry. He was matter-of-fact, candid, even funny at times. He told me that his wife liked him better the way he was.

"I don't run around," he explained. "It's not that I can't . . . the ladies, they don't seem to mind the way I am. In fact, they seem to like it. I just don't want to, I don't feel like a man."

"So the marriage is better?"

He shrugged. "She's a prude. She'd rather not have sex anyway. So how about a hormone shot, Doc? What do we got to lose?"

His optimism was infectious, and I gave him a shot of testosterone. And another a few weeks later. It didn't change anything. The next time I saw him he was carrying a newspaper clipping.

"I heard about this operation," he said, handing me the article. "They got something they put in your penis to make it hard. A metal rod, something like that. They also got this tube they can put in. With a pump, so you can pump it up when you're ready and let it down when you're finished. What do you think, Doc?"

I knew a little about the implants. The rods were okay, except the penis stayed stiff all the time. It was a nuisance, and sometimes it hurt if it got bent the wrong way. The inflatable tubes were unreliable, sometimes breaking open, other times not deflating when they were supposed to. I told him this.

"It's worth a try," he said. "What do I got to lose?"

It was four or five months before I saw him again. He couldn't wait to get me in the examining room, pulling down his pants almost as soon as I shut the door. Through the slit in his underwear his penis pointed at me like a finger. His face beamed.

"I can go for hours now, Doc," he said proudly. "Six, eight, all night if I want. And look at his . . ." He bent it to the right, where it stayed, nearly touching his leg. Then to the left. Then straight up, then down. "Any position, for as long as I want. The women, they love it."

I sat there, marvelling. "That's great."

"You should see them," he said, bending it down in the shape of a question mark and stuffing it back in his pants. "They go crazy. I'm like a kid, Doc. They can't keep up with me."

I thought of him, sixty-two years old, happy, stiff, rolling back and forth on an old mattress, stopping every so often to ask his companion that night which way she wanted it. Did she like it better left or right, curved or straight, up or down? He was a man now, and he loved women. I asked about his wife.

"She wants to divorce me," he said. "I got too many women now."

The question, I think, is not so much what I have in common with the banded krait of India, him slithering through the mud of that ancient country's monsoon-swollen rivers, me sitting pensively in a cardigan at my desk. We share that certain sequence of nucleic acids, that gene on the Y chromosome that makes us male. The snake is aggressive; I am loyal and dependable. He is territorial; I am a faithful family man. He dominates the female of his species; I am strong, reliable, a good lover.

The question really is how I differ from my wife. We lay in bed, our long bodies pressed together as though each of us were trying to become the other. We talk, sometimes of love, mostly of problems. She says, my job, it is so hard, I am so tired my body aches. And I think, that is too bad, I am so sorry, where is the money to come from, be tough, buck up. I say, I am insecure at work, worried about being a good father, a husband. And she says, you are good, I love you, which washes off me as though she had said the sky is blue. She strokes my head and I feel trapped; I stroke hers and she purrs like a cat. What is this? I ask, nervous, frightened. Love, she says. Kiss me.

I am still so baffled. It is not as simple as the brains of rats. As a claw, a fang, a battlefield scarred with bodies. I want to possess, and be possessed.

One night she said to me, "I think men and women are two different species."

It was late. We were close, not quite touching. "Maybe soon," I said. "Not yet."

"It might be better." She yawned. "It would certainly be easier."

I took her hand and squeezed it. "That's why we cling so hard to one another."

She snuggled up to me. "We like it."

I sighed. "It's because we know someday we may not want to cling at all."

References:

[1] Wachtel, Stephen: *H-Y Antigen and the Biology of Sex Determination*, New York, Grune & Stratton, 1983, p. 170.

[2] Ibid, p. 172.

[3] Gordon, H., in Vallet, HL & Porter, IH (eds): *Genetic Mechanisms of Sexual Development*, New York, Academic Press, 1979, p. 18.

[4] Rudolf, IE, et al.: *Whither the Male?: Studies in Functionally Split Identities*, Philadelphia, Ova Press, 1982.

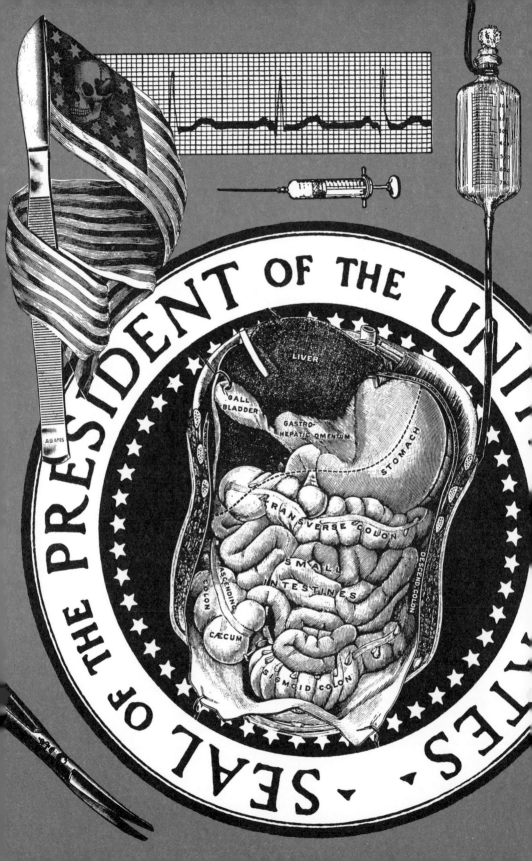

TISSUE ABLATION AND VARIANT REGENERATION: A CASE REPORT

At seven a.m. on Thursday morning Mr. Reagan was wheeled through the swinging doors and down the corridor to operating room six. He was lying flat on the gurney, and his gaze was fixed on the ceiling; he had the glassy stare of a man in shock. I was concerned that he had been given analgesia, but the attendant assured me that he had not. As we were talking, Mr. Reagan turned his eyes to me: the pupils were wide, dark as olives, and I recognized the dilatation of pain and fear. I felt sympathy, but more, I was relieved that he had not inadvertently been narcotized, for it would have delayed the operation for days.

I had yet to scrub and placed my hand on his shoulder to acknowledge his courage. His skin was coarse beneath the thin sheet that covered him, as the pili erecti tried in vain to warm the chill we had induced. He shivered, which was natural, though eventually it would stop — it must — if we were to proceed with the surgery. I removed my hand and bent to examine the plastic bag that hung like a showy organ from the side of the gurney. There was nearly a liter of pale urine, which assured me that his kidneys were functioning well.

I turned away, and, entering the scrub room, once more conceptualized our plan. There were three teams, one for each pair of extremities and a third for torso and viscera. I headed the latter, which was proper, for the major responsibility for this project

was mine. We had chosen to avoid analgesia, the analeptic properties of excruciating pain being well known. There are several
well-drawn studies that conclusively demonstrate the superior
survival of tissues thus exposed, and I have cited these in a number of my own monographs. In addition, chlorinated hydrocar-
bons, which still form the bulk of our anesthetics, are tissue-toxic
in extremely small quantities. Though these agents clear rapidly
in the normal course of post-operative recovery, tissue propaga-
tion is too sensitive a phenomenon for us to have risked their use.
The patient was offered, routinely, the choice of an Eastern mode
of anesthesia, but he demurred. Mr. Reagan has an obdurate
faith in things American.

I set the timer above the sink and commenced to scrub.
Through the window I watched as the staff went about the final
preparations. Two large tables stood along one wall, and on top
of them sat the numerous trays of instruments we would use during the operation. Since this was the largest one of its kind any of
us at the center had participated in, I had been generous in my
estimation of what would be needed. It is always best in such
situations to err on the side of caution, and I had ordered dupli-
cates of each pack to be prepared and placed accessibly. Already
an enormous quantity of instruments lay unpacked on the tables,
divided into general areas of proximity. Thus, urologic was
placed beside rectal and lower intestinal, and hepatic, splenic,
and gastric were grouped together. Thoracic was separate, and
orthopedic and vascular were divided into two groups for those
teams assigned to the extremities. There were three sets of general
instruments — hemostats, forceps, scissors, and the like — and
these were on smaller trays that stood close to the operating table.
Perched above them, and sorting the instruments chronologi-
cally, were the scrub nurses, hooded, masked, and gloved. Behind, and throughout the operating room circulated other, non-
sterile personnel, the nurses and technicians who functioned as
the extended arm of the team.

For the dozenth time I scrubbed my cuticles and the space

between fingernail and fingertip, then scoured both sides of my forearms to the elbow. The sheet had been removed from Mr. Reagan, and his ventral surface — from neck to foot — was covered by the yellow suds of antiseptic. His pubic parts, chest, and axilla, had been shaved earlier, although he had no great plethora of hair to begin with. The artificial light striking his body at that moment recalled to me the jaundiced hue I have seen at times on certain dysfunctional gall bladders, and I looked at my own hands. They seemed brighter, and I rinsed them several times, then backed into the surgical suite.

A nurse approached with a towel, whose corner I grabbed, proceeding to dry methodically each finger. She returned with a glove, spreading the entrance wide as one might the mouth of a fish in order to peer down its throat. I thrust my fingers and thumb into it and she snapped it upon my forearm. She repeated the exchange with the other, and I thanked her, then stood back and waited for the final preparations.

The soap had been removed from his skin, and now Mr. Reagan was being draped with various sized linens. Two of these were used to fashion a vertical barrier at the mid-point of his neck; behind this, with his head, sat the two anesthesiologists. Since no anesthetic was to be used, their responsibility lay in monitoring his respiratory and cardiovascular status. He would be intubated, and they would make periodic measurements of the carbon dioxide and oxygen content of his blood.

I gave them a nod and they inserted the intracath, through which we would drip a standard, paralytic dose of succinylcholine. We had briefly considered doing without the drug, for its effect, albeit minimal, would still be noticeable on the ablated tissues. Finally, though, we had chosen to use it, reasoning — and experience proved us correct — that we could not rely on the paralysis of pain to immobilize the patient for the duration of the surgery. If there had been a lull, during which time he had chosen to move, hours of careful work might have been destroyed. Prudence dictated a conservative approach.

After initiating the paralytic, Dr. Guevara, the senior anesthesiologist, promptly inserted the endotracheal tube. It passed easily for there was little, if any, muscular resistance. The respirator was turned on and artificial ventilation begun. I told Mr. Reagan, who would be conscious throughout, that we were about to begin.

I stepped to the table and surveyed the body. The chest was exposed, as were the two legs, above which Drs. Ng and Cochise were poised to begin.

"Scalpel," I said, and the tool was slapped into my palm. I transferred it to my other hand. "Forceps."

I bent over the body, mentally drawing a line from the sternal notch to the symphysis pubis. We had studied our approaches for hours, for the incisions were unique and had been used but rarely before. A procedure of this scale required precision in every detail in order that we preserve the maximal amount of viable tissue. I lifted the scalpel and with a firm and steady hand made the first cut.

He had been cooled in part to cause constriction of the small dermal vessels, thus reducing the quantity of blood lost to ooze. We were not, of course, able to use the electric scalpel to cut or coagulate, nor could we tie bleeding vessels, for both would inflict damage to tissue. Within reason, we had chosen planes incision that avoided major dermal vasculature, and as I retraced my first cut, pressing harder to separate the more stubborn fascial layers, I was reassured by the paucity of blood that was appearing at the margins of the wound. I exchanged my delicate tissue forceps for a larger pair, everting the stratum of skin, fat, and muscle, and continuing my incision until I reached the costochondral junction in the chest and the linea alba in the belly. I made two lateral incisions, one from the pubis, along the inguinal ligament, ending near the anterior superior iliac spine, and the other from the sternal notch, along the inferior border of the clavicle to the anterior edge of the axilla. There was more blood appearing now, and for a moment I aided Dr. Biko in packing the wound. Much of our success at controlling the bleeding depended, however, upon the speed at which I carried out the next stage, and with this in mind, I left him to mop the red fluid and turned to the thorax.

Pectus hypertrophicus occurs perhaps in one in a thousand; Billings, in a recent study of a dozen such cases, links the condition to a congenital aberration of the short arm of chromosome thirteen, and he postulates a correlation between the hypertrophied sternum, a marked preponderance of glabrous skin, and a mild associative cortical defect. He has studied these cases; I have not. Indeed, Mr. Reagan's sternum was only the second in all my experience that would not yield to the Lebsche knife. I asked for the bone snips, and with the help of Dr. Biko was finally able to split the structure. My forehead dripped from the effort, and a circulating nurse dabbed it with a towel.

I applied the wide-armed retractor, and as I ratcheted it apart, I felt a wince of resistance. I asked Dr. Guevara to increase the infusion of muscle relaxant, for we were entering a most crucial part of the operation.

"His pupils are fixed and dilated," he announced.

I could see his heart, and it was beating normally. "His gases?" I asked.

"O_2 85, CO_2 38, pH 7.37."

"Good," I said. "It's just agony then. Not death." Dr. Guevara nodded above the barrier that separated us, and as he bent to whisper words of encouragement to Mr. Reagan, I looked into the chest. There I paused, as I always seem to do at the sight of that glistening organ. It throbbed and rolled, sensuously, I thought, majestically, and I renewed my vows to treat it kindly. With the tissue forceps I lifted the pericardium and with the curved scissors punctured it. It peeled off smoothly, reminding me fleetingly of the delicate skin that encloses the tip of the male child's penis.

In rapid succession I ligated the inferior vena cava and cross-clamped the descending aorta, just distal to the bronchial arteries. We had decided not to use our bypass system, thus obviating cannulations that would have required lengthy and meticulous suturing. We had opted instead for a complete de-vascularization distal to the thoracic cavity, reasoning that since all the organs and other structures were to be removed anyway, there was no sense in preserving circulation below the heart. I signalled to my colleagues waiting at the lower extremities to begin their dissections.

I isolated the right subclavian artery and vein, ligated them, and did the same on the left. I anastomosed the internal thoracic artery to the ventral surface of the aortic arch, thus providing arterial flow to the chest wall, which we planned to preserve more or less intact. I returned to the descending aorta, choosing 3-0 Ethilon to assure occlusion of the lumen, and oversewed twice. I released the clamp slowly: there was no leakage, and I breathed a sigh of satisfaction. We had completed a crucial stage, isolating the thoracic and cephalic circulation from that of the rest of the body, and the patient's condition remained stable. What was left was the harvesting of his parts.

I would like to insert here a word on our behalf, aimed not just at the surgical team but at the full technical and administrative apparatus. We had early on agreed that we must approach the dissection assiduously, meaning that in every case we would apply a greater, rather than a lesser, degree of scrupulousness. At the time of the operation no use — other than in transplantation — had been found for many of the organs we were to resect. Such parts as colon, spleen, and vasculature had not then, nor have they yet, struck utilitarian chords in our imaginations. Surely, they will in the future, and with this as our philosophy we determined to discard not even the most seemingly insignificant part. What could not immediately be utilized would be preserved in our banks, waiting for a bright idea to send it to the regeneration tanks.

It was for this reason, and this reason alone, that the operation lasted as long as it did. I would be lying if I claimed that Mr. Reagan was not in constant and excruciating pain. Who would not be to have his skin fileted, his chest cracked, his limbs meticulously dissected and dismembered? In retrospect, I should have carried out a high transection of the spinal cord, thus interrupting most of the nerve fibers to his brain, but I did not think of it beforehand and during the operation was too occupied with other concerns. That he did survive is a testimony to his strength, though I still remember his post-operative shrieks and protestations. We had, of course, already detached his upper limbs, and therefore we ourselves had to dab the streams of tears that flew from his eyes. At that point, there being no further danger of tissue damage, I did order an analgesic.

After I had successfully completed the de-vascularization procedure, thus removing the risk of life-threatening hemorrhage from our fields, I returned to the outer layer of thorax and abdomen. With an Adson forceps I gently retracted the thin sheet of dermis and began to undermine with the scalpel. It was painstaking, but after much time I finally had the entire area freed. It hung limp, drooping like a dewlap, and as I began the final axillary cut that would release it completely, I asked Ms. Narciso, my scrub nurse, to call the technician. He came just as I finished, and I handed him the skin.

I confess that I have less than a full understanding of the technology of organ variation and regeneration. I am a surgeon, not a technologist, and devote the major part of my energies toward refinement and perfection of operative skills. We do, however, live in an age of great scientific achievement, and the iconoclasm of many of my younger colleagues has forced me to cast my gaze more broadly afield. Thus it is that I am not a complete stranger to inductive mitotics and controlled oncogenesis, and I will attempt to convey the fundamentals.

Upon receiving the tissue, the technician transports it to the appropriate room wherein lie the thermo-magnetic protein baths. These are organ specific, distinguished by temperature, pH, magnetic field, and substrate, and designed to suppress cellular activity; specifically, they prolong dormancy at the G1 stage of mitosis. The magnetic field is altered then, such that each cell will arrange itself ninety degrees to it. A concentrated solution of isotonic nucleic and amino acids is then pumped into the tank, and the bath mechanically agitated to diffuse the solute. Several hours are allowed to pass, and the magnetic field is again shifted, attempting to align it with the nucleic loci that govern the latter stages of mitosis. If this is successful, and success is immediately apparent for failure induces rapid and massive necrosis, the organ system will begin to reproduce. This is a macroscopic phenomenon, obvious to the naked eye. I have been present at this critical moment, and it is a simple, yet wondrous, thing to behold.

Different organs regenerate, multiply, in distinctive fashion. In the case of the skin, genesis occurs quite like the polymerization of synthetic fibers, such as nylon and its congeners. The testes grow in a more sequential manner, analogous perhaps to the clustering of grapes along the vine. Muscles seem to laminate, forming thicker and thicker sheets until, if not separated, they collapse upon themselves. Bone propagates as tubules; ligaments, as lianoid strands of great length. All distinct, yet all variations on a theme.

In the case of our own patient, the outcome, I am pleased to report, was bounteous; this was especially gratifying in light of our guarded prognostications. I was not alone in the skepticism with which I approached the operation, for the tissues and regenerative capacity of an old man are not those of a youngster. During the surgery, when I noticed the friability and general degree of degeneration of his organs, my thoughts were inclined rather pessimistically. I remember wondering, as Dr. Cochise severed the humeral head from the glenoid fossa, inadvertently crushing a quantity of porotic and fragile bone, if our scrupulous planning had not been a waste of effort, that the fruits of our labor would not be commensurate with our toil. Even now, with the benefit of hindsight, I remain astonished at our degree of success. As much as it is a credit to the work of our surgical team, it is, perhaps moreso, a tribute to the resilience and fundamental vitality of the human body.

After releasing the dermal layer as described, I proceeded to detach the muscles. The adipose tissue, so slippery and difficult to manipulate, would be removed chemically, thus saving valuable time. As I have mentioned, the risk of hemorrhage — and its threat to Mr. Reagan's life — had been eliminated, but because of the resultant interruption of circulation we were faced with the real possibility of massive tissue necrosis. For this reason we were required to move most expeditiously.

With sweeping, but well guided strokes of the scalpel I transected the ligamentous origins of Pectoralis Major and Minor, and Serratus Anterior. I located their points of insertion on the scapula and humerus and severed them as well, indicating to Ms. Narciso that we would need the technician responsible for the muscles. She replied that he had already been summoned by Dr. Ng, and I took that moment to peer in his vicinity.

He and Dr. Cochise had been working rapidly, already having completed the spiraling circumferential incisions from groin to toe, thus allowing, in a fashion similar to the peeling of an orange, the removal in toto of the dermal sheath of the leg. The anterior femoral and pelvic musculature had been exposed, and I could see the Sartorius and at least two of the Quadriceps heads dangling. This was good work and I nodded appreciatively, then turned my attention to the abdominal wall.

In terms of time the abdominal muscles presented less of a problem than the thoracic ones, for there were no ribs to contend with. In addition, as long as I was careful not to puncture the viscera, I could enter the peritoneum almost recklessly. I took my scalpel and thrust it upon the xiphoid, near what layman call the solar plexus, and started the long and penetrating incision down the linea alba, past the umbilicus, to the symphysis pubis. With one hand I lifted the margin of the wound, and with the other delicately sliced the peritoneal membrane. I reflected all the abdominal muscles, the Rectus and Transversus Abdominis, the

Obliquus Internus and Externus, and detached them from their bony insertions. Grasping the peritoneum with a long-toothed forceps and peeling it back, I placed two large towel clips in the overlying muscle mass, and then, as an iceman would pick up a block of ice, lifted it above the table, passing it into the hands of the waiting technician. Another was there for the thoracic musculature, and once these were cleared from the table, I turned to the abdominal contents themselves.

Let me interject a note as to the status of our patient at that time. As deeply as I become involved in the techniques and mechanics of any surgery, I am always, with another part of my mind, aware of the human being who lies at the mercy of the knife. At this juncture in our operation I noticed, by the flaccidity in the muscles on the other half of the abdomen, that the patient was perhaps too deeply relaxed. Always there is a tension in the muscles, and this must be mollified sufficiently to allow the surgeon to operate without undo resistance, but not so much that it endangers the life of the patient. In this case I noted little, if any, resistance, and I asked Dr. Guevara to reduce slightly the rate of infusion of the relaxant. This affected all the muscles, including, of course, the diaphragm and those of the larynx, and Mr. Reagan took the opportunity to attempt to vocalize. Being intubated, he was in no position to do so, yet somehow managed to produce a keening sound that unnerved us all. His face, as reported by Dr. Guevara, became constricted in a horrible rictus, and his eyes seemed to convulse in their sockets. Clearly, he was in excruciating pain, and my heart flew to him as to a valiant soldier.

The agony, I am certain, was not simply corporeal; surely there was a psychological aspect to it, perhaps a psychosis, as he thought upon the systematic dissection and dismemberment of his manifest self. To me, I know it would have been unbearable, and once again I was humbled by his courage and fortitude. And yet there was still so much left to do; neither empathy nor despair were distractions we could afford. Accordingly, I asked Dr. Guevara to increase the infusion rate in order to still Mr. Reagan's cries, and this achieved, I returned my concentration to the table.

By prearrangement Dr. Biko now moved to the opposite side of the patient and began to duplicate there what I had just finished on mine. The sole modification was that he began on the belly wall and proceeded in a cephalad direction, so that by the time I had extirpated the contents of one half of the abdomen, the other would be exposed and ready. With alacrity I began the evisceration.

It would be tedious to chronicle step by step the various dissections, ligations, and severances; these are detailed in a separate monograph, whose reference can be found in the bibliography. Suffice to say that I identified the organs and proceeded with the resections as we had planned. Once freeing the stomach, I was able to remove the spleen and pancreas without much delay. Because of their combined mass, the liver and gall bladder required more time but eventually came out quite nicely. I reflected the proximal small and large intestines downward in order to lay bare the deeper recesses of the upper abdominal cavity and have access to the kidneys and adrenals. I treated gland and organ as a unit, removing each pair together, transecting the ureters high, near the renal pelvices. The big abdominal vessels, vena cava and aorta, were now exposed, and I had to withstand the urge to include them in my dissection. We had previously agreed that this part of the procedure would be assumed by Dr. Biko, who is as skilled and renowned a vascular surgeon as I am an abdomino-thoracic one, and though they lay temptingly now within my reach, I resisted the lure and turned to accomplish the extirpation of the alimentary tract.

We did not, as many had urged, remove the cavitous segment of the digestive apparatus as a whole. After consultation with our technical staff we determined that it would be more practical and successful if we proceeded segmentally. Thus, we divided the tract into three parts: stomach, including the esophageal segment just distal to the diaphragm; small intestine, from pylorus to ileo-cecal valve; and colon, from cecum to anus. These were dutifully resected and sent to the holding banks, where they await future purpose and need.

As I harvested the internal abdominal musculature, the Psoas, Iliacus, Quadratus Lumborum, I let my mind wander for a few moments. We were nearing the end of the operation, and I felt the luxury of certain philosophical meditations. I thought about the people of the world, the hungry, the cold, those without shelter or goods to meet the exigencies of daily life. What are our responsibilities to them, we the educated, the skilled, the possessors? It is said, and I believe, that no man stands above any other. What then can one person do for the many? Listen, I suppose. Change.

I have found in my profession, as I am certain exists in all others, that to not adapt is to become obsolete. I have known many colleagues, who, unwilling or unable to grapple with innovation, have gone the way of the penny. Tenacity, in some an admirable quality, is no substitute for the ability to change, for what in one age might be considered tenacious in another would most certainly be called cowardly. I thought upon our patient, whose fortunes had so altered since the years of my training, and considered further the question of justice. Could an act of great altruism, albeit forced and involuntary, balance a generation of infamy? How does the dedication of one's own body to the masses weigh upon the scales of sin and repentance?

My brow furrowed, for these questions were far more difficult to me than the operation itself, and had it not been for Ms. Narciso, who spoke up in a timely voice, I might have broken the sterile field by wiping with my own hand the perspiration on my forehead.

"Shall we move to the pelvis, Doctor?" she said, breaking my reverie.

"Yes," I replied softly, turning momentarily from the table to recover, while a nurse mopped the moist skin of my face.

The bladder, of course, had been decompressed by the catheter that had been passed prior to surgery, and once I pierced the floor of the peritoneum, it lay beneath my blade like a flat and flaccid tire. I severed it quickly, taking care to include the prostate, seminal vesicles, ureters, and membranous urethra in the resection. A technician carried these to an intermediate room, where a surgeon was standing by to separate the structures before they were taken to their respective tanks. What remained was to take the penis, which was relatively simple, and testes, which required more care so as not to disrupt the delicate tunica that surrounded them. This done, I straightened my back for perhaps the first time since we began and assessed our progress.

When one becomes so engrossed in a task, so keyed and focussed that huge chunks of time pass unaware, it is a jarring feeling, akin to waking from a vivid and lifelike dream, to return to reality. I have felt this frequently during surgeries, but never as I did this time. Hours had passed, personnel had changed, perhaps even the moon outside had risen, in a span that for me was marked in moments. I looked for Drs. Ng and Cochise and was informed that they had left the surgical suite some time ago. I recalled this only dimly, but when I looked to their work was pleased to find that it had been performed most adequately. All limbs were gone, and the glenoid fossae, where the shoulders had been de-articulated, were sealed as we had discussed. Across from me Dr. Biko was just completing the abdominal vascular work. I nodded to myself, and using an interior approach, detached the muscles of the lumbar spine, then asked for the bone saw.

We transected the spinal cord between the second and third lumbar vertebrae, thus preserving the major portion of attachments of the diaphragm. This, of course, was vital, if, as we had planned, Mr. Reagan was to retain the ability to respire. It is well-known that those who leave surgery still attached to the respirator, which surely would have been the case if we had been sloppy in this last part of the operation, do poorly thereafter, often dying in the immediate post-operative period. In this case especially, such an outcome would have been particularly heinous, for it would have deprived this brave man of the fate and rewards most deservedly his.

I am nearing the conclusion of our report, and it must be obvious that I have failed to include each and every nerve, ligament, muscle, and vessel that we removed. If it seems a critical error, I can only say that it is a purposeful one, intended to improve the readability of this document. Hopefully, I have made it more accessible to the lay that exist outside the cloister of our medical world, but those who crave more detailed information I refer to the *Archives of Ablative Technique*, vol. 113, number 6, pp. 67-104, or, indeed, to any comprehensive atlas of anatomy.

We sealed the chest wall and sub-diaphragmatic area with a synthetic polymer (XRO 137, by Dow) that is thin but surprisingly durable and impervious to bacterial invasion. We did a towel count to make certain that none were inadvertently left inside the patient, though at that point there was little of him that could escape our attention, then Dr. Guevara inserted the jugular catheter that would be used for nourishment and medication. Dr. Biko fashioned a neat little fistula from the right external carotid artery, which, because we had taken the kidneys, would be used for dialysis. These completed, we did a final blood gas and vital sign check, each of which was acceptable, and I stepped back from the table.

"Thank you all very much," I said, and turned to Mr. Reagan as I peeled back my gloves. He was beginning to recover from the drug-induced paralysis, and his face seemed to recoil from mine as I bent toward him. I have seen this before in surgery, where the strange apparel, the hooded and masked faces, often cause fright in a patient. It is especially common in the immediate post-operative period, when unusual bodily sensations and a frequently marked mental disorientation play such large roles. I was therefore not alarmed to see our patient's features contort as I drew near.

"It is over," I said gently, keeping my words simple and clear. "It went well. We will take the tube from your mouth, but don't try to talk. Your throat will be quite sore for awhile, and it will hurt."

I placed a hand on his cheek, which felt clammy even though the skin was flushed, and Dr. Guevara withdrew the tube. By that time the muscle relaxant had worn off completely, and Mr. Reagan responded superbly by beginning to breathe on his own immediately. Shortly thereafter, he began to shriek.

There are some surgeons I know, and many other physicians, who believe in some arcane manner in the strengthening properties of pain. They assert that it fortifies the organism, steeling it, as it were, to the insults of disease. Earlier, I mentioned the positive association between pain and tissue survival, but this obtains solely with respect to ablative surgery. It has not been demonstrated under myriad other circumstances, and this despite literally hundreds of studies to prove it so. The only possible conclusion, the only scientific one, is that pain, apart from its value as a mechanism of warning, has none of those attributes the algophilists ascribe to it. In my mind these practitioners are reprehensible moralists and should be barred from those specialties, such as surgery, where the problem is ubiquitous.

Needless to say, as soon as Mr. Reagan began to cry, I ordered a potent and long-lasting analgesic. For the first time since we began his face quieted and his eyes closed, and though I never questioned him on it, I like to think that his dreams were sweet and proud at what he, one man, had been able to offer thousands.

Save for the appendix, this is the whole of my report. Once again I apologize for omissions and refer the interested reader to the ample bibliography. We have demonstrated, I believe, the viability of extensive tissue ablation and its value in providing substrate for inductive and variant mitotics. Although it is an arduous undertaking, I believe it holds promise for selected patients in the future.

Appendix

As of the writing of this document, the following items and respective quantities have been produced by our regeneration systems:

Item	Source	Quantity
Oil, refined	Testes: seminiferous tubules	3761 liters
Perfumes and scents	Same	162 grams
Meat, including patties, filets, and ground round	Muscles	13,318 kilograms
Storage jugs	Bladder	2732
Balls, inflatable (recreational use)	Same	325
Cord, multi-purposed	Ligaments	1.2 kilometers
Roofing material, e.g., for tents; flexible siding	Skin: full thickness	3.6 sq. kilometers
Prophylactics	Skin: stratum granulosum	18,763 cartons of 10 ea.
Various enzymes, medications, hormones	Pancreas, adrenal glands, hepatic tissue	272 grams
Flexible struts and housing supports	Bone	453 sq. meters

The vast majority of these have been distributed, principally to countries of the third world, but also to impoverished areas of our own nation. A follow-up study to update our data and provide a geographical breakdown by item will be conducted within the year.

THE DOMINO MASTER

I first met Jake the night my father came home all drunk. My mother was drunk too and they yelled at each other, and then she hit him over the head with a bottle. His hair got red and blood started coming over his face and eyes. She screamed, and I got scared. She ran to help him, and I ran out of the apartment.

When I got to the stairs I stopped. I wasn't supposed to go out by myself, but I couldn't go back. I took a deep breath and stepped on the first step. When nothing happened, I took another. Suddenly, the door at the top of the stairs opened. I froze. Then a cat came out.

It was a tired-looking cat, black and white, with the longest fur I'd ever seen. It yawned and trotted off down the stairs. The door stayed open, and suddenly, a face appeared in the crack. It had old looking eyes and whiskers, but it wasn't much higher than a kid.

"Stupid cat," it said. "You'd think he'd know by now." He looked at me. "Wouldn't you think he'd know?"

I stared at him. I didn't know what he was talking about, and besides, I wasn't supposed to talk to strangers. Especially not if this was the man who lived at the end of the hall.

"*You* know," he kept on. "You're the right size. I'm sure you know." He shook his head. "You'd think a cat would. Especially that cat."

"Know what?"

"Maybe he's just too old. I know he knows. Maybe he just can't do anything about it."

"About what? What, Mister?"

He looked at me and blinked. He had gray eyebrows and mussed-up gray hair on the sides of his head. The top was bald.

"Come in and see for yourself. See what you think. Then you tell me."

He disappeared and the door opened wider. Everything inside looked orange. Some kind of song was playing but I couldn't hear exactly what. I took a step toward the door, then stopped. I listened.

"The ants go marching one by one, hurrah, hurrah. The ants go marching one by one, hurrah, hurrah. The ants go marching one by one, the little one stops to have some fun . . ." I knew the song from school and went inside to hear more.

As soon as I got in, I saw him again. He was kneeling on a rug inside the door, staring at it and looking glum. If this was the man who lived in the apartment, he didn't seem so scary to me. In fact he seemed kind of sad.

I went over, but when I got close he put out a hand.

"Hold it," he said. "You don't want to step in it." He shook his head. "Stupid cat. My favorite carpet too."

I looked down. It was dark but not too dark to see the stain on the rug.

"Is that it, Mister?"

"Jake," he said.

"Is that it, Mister Jake? Is that what your cat did?"

"Not my cat. Not mine. Sometimes I wish it were, but of course it isn't. Can't be. Or couldn't."

"Huh?"

He looked at me. "Don't be simple, boy. You know as well as I do what that cat did. Would you do that on your rug?"

I stared at him, a little but not too scared, and shook my head.

"Of course you wouldn't. You've got manners."

"Sometimes I wet my bed."

"Of course you do. Sometimes I do too. But not the rug. Not that. Stupid cat."

"Maybe it didn't mean to. Maybe it was just a mistake."

He opened his mouth to say something but then shut it. He sighed and sat back on his heels.

"You're very wise, my friend. It *was* a mistake, that's the sad part."

"My name's Johnny."

"When you wet the bed, it's a part of growing up. When we do, it's a sign of growing down." He ran his fingers through the bunches of hair above his ears. "Poor cat."

"I'll help you clean it up. I know how."

"Do you?" That seemed to perk him up. "By all means, then, help."

"I need some salt."

He pushed himself up and left the room. In a minute he came back with an old glass jar with the letters NaCl written across the front. He took off the top and handed the jar to me.

"This is it?"

"From the Dead Sea itself, John. I may call you that, if I may. May I?"

I shrugged and poured the salt on the spot. Pretty soon it got caked up and the yellow began to show through, so I poured out more. By the time I finished nearly the whole jar was gone.

"Quite a handy little man, aren't you? I must tell Arsenio your trick. He would want to know."

"Who's he?"

"A little friend. I'm sure you'll meet him, or rather I'm not sure, but you might. But here . . ." He got up again, I guess because he saw that his rug was going to be okay, and took my hand. Then he started to march. Up and down went his legs, and then he started to sing.

"The ants go marching one by one, hurrah, hurrah. The ants

go marching one by one, then John he comes to have some fun, and they all go marching round, and around, to get out of the rain, Boom, Boom, Boom . . ."

I joined in, and in a minute the two of us were in the orange room, marching around and around, singing and clapping every time we came to the "Boom, Boom, Boom." When we got to ten we went through the whole song again, which no grown-up ever did with me before. After the second time we stopped. Jake was breathing hard, too hard I guess to keep going. He went to the side of the room and flopped down on a stack of pillows on the floor. He stuck out his legs and closed his eyes. I waited for something to happen. When nothing did, I decided to look around.

At first it seemed like the room was full of junk. Things were hanging all over the place, from the walls and tables and even over the backs of chairs. There was stuff piled up high on the floor, and boxes everywhere. I thought what my Mom would do if my room ever looked like that, but then I stopped thinking about it because I didn't want to. Instead I looked at the boxes.

All of them were long and skinny, all kind of the same but different. Some of them shined bright like the sun and some were so dark you couldn't even see what was on them. On top of one were drawings of funny looking animals, almost but not quite like ones at the zoo. One was a horse with a tail and everything, but also it had wings. There was another horse too, but that one had the face of a woman with long hair, kind of like a girl I knew from school. And there was a dragon on the box, and a bird flying up out of a big fire. I liked looking at it, but also it seemed stupid to have animals that weren't really animals. So I stopped looking and went to another box.

This one was blue and bright. It flashed on and off like the police lights when they run their sirens. I wanted to open it but I couldn't figure out how. So I picked it up.

Some things rattled inside, which scared me. Real fast I put it down and walked away. I didn't want Jake to know that I even touched it.

Luckily, his eyes were still closed. I couldn't tell if he was asleep or awake, and I went over to see. The room was so crowded that by mistake I bumped into a table. It hurt my leg, and I stooped over to rub it. Then I saw the box on top.

It was the blackest black I had ever seen, blacker even than my friend Joey's birthmark on his face. It was so black it seemed like it wasn't even there, like a hole or something. I put out my hand to see if it was real, and then all of a sudden Jake woke up.

"Don't touch that!" he said. I jerked my hand back and looked at him.

"Good boy." He leaned over and snatched the box away, stuffing it behind one of the pillows.

"How about some milk? Little boys like milk."

I shook my head. "I gotta go home."

"Of course you do. How could I be so sleepy? Your parents must be worried."

He smiled and reached into one of his pockets. He held out something in his hand.

"Here. It's a present."

I wasn't supposed to, but it didn't seem anything bad. So I took it. It was a pin, and attached to one side were two white squares joined together by a black line in the middle. On each square were some black dots.

"A domino," he said. "Can you put it on yourself?"

I nodded and showed him. Then I turned around and went home.

I didn't see him again for a long time, but I didn't stop thinking about him. Especially that black box which he snatched away from me. I would've gone back sooner, except that after that night my Mom moved out of our apartment and took me with her. We moved to her friend Ginny's place, which was even smaller than ours. After awhile Ginny said that we had to leave, it was just too crowded. Mom said it was okay because by then she and Dad were seeing each other again. They were back in love, she said.

Dad said the same thing when I saw him. He gave me a big

hug, which hurt a little. "Welcome back, Johnny boy," he said. He cooked us all a big breakfast, eggs and toast and pancakes, and he gave me a new GI Joe. He gave Mom a real short nightgown and after breakfast they told me to play by myself for awhile. They went into the bedroom, locked the door and started giggling. I knew what that meant so I went and turned on the TV. But it was broke, so I played with Joe. He was okay but after awhile I got tired of him because all he wanted to do was hit the other soldiers and make them bleed on their heads. I thought about Jake. And the box.

From the noise they were making I figured Mom and Dad wouldn't miss me. So I told Joe not to tell, and the other guys, and I tiptoed out the door and down the hall.

When I got to Jake's, I looked around for a button to push but there wasn't one. There wasn't a doorknob either. I was afraid to knock because of the noise, and I didn't know what to do. Then I heard music.

It was faraway and real soft. I shut my eyes and leaned against the door. I listened hard. The song was just starting on four.

"The ants go marching four by four, hurrah, hurrah. The ants go marching four by four, the little one stops to knock at the door . . ." And all of a sudden I found myself knocking at Jake's door. Nothing happened, and I knocked again. And the door, without even the smallest creak, opened.

"Come in, come in," a voice said and right away I knew it was him. I went in and the door shut behind me. I walked through the little hall into the orange room.

"Hi," I said when I saw him, and he waved me in. He was lying on the pillows, looking the same as before except for the pipe in his mouth. It was a long one, almost as long as his whole body. It was so long in fact that he could hardly light it, which he was trying to do with a long, skinny match. By the time he got his hand steady enough to put the flame over the bowl of the pipe, the match had burned down so much that he had to move his hand again. He kept having to stretch out farther and farther. Finally, he got the pipe smoking, but then the match went out. He groaned and looked at me.

"I'd use pyrotechnics, but I might burn down the house. Give me a hand, will you?"

I went over and stood next to him.

"A hand," he said. "You've got ears, haven't you?" I held one out, a hand I mean, and he lit a match and gave it to me.

"Now put it there. Over the bowl."

I did what he told me and he began to puff. The stuff in the bowl glowed red and then he took the pipe out of his mouth and blew out the match.

"I could do that," I said.

He looked at me while he had some more puffs. Then he took the match and began rubbing its tip between his finger and thumb. He stopped, and in a second it burst into flame.

I stared. It was such a great trick that I forgot about blowing the match out. Just before it burned his fingers I remembered, and blew. He looked at me.

"I apologize if I'm a bit out of sorts," he said, "but the cat went and did it again. It seems as though your visits trigger something in him."

"I didn't do anything, Mister Jake. Honest."

"Of course you didn't. And it's just Jake."

"I can clean it up. Like before."

"I've already taken care of it. Or rather Arsenio has. Or is. He should be just about finished."

Before I could ask who Arsenio was, a kid came walking into the room. He was smaller than me and looked rich, like one of those kids you see sometimes in the store getting their hair done up just like they were a grown-up. His was slicked down and shiny, and parted right down the middle. It made him look funny. He had on dark pants and a matching jacket, and black shoes that were as shiny as his hair. To top it off he was wearing a bow-tie, which I had never seen anyone except old men on the street wear. He looked like a picture of a guy I'd seen once in a museum, except he wasn't a guy but a kid.

"Arsenio," Jake said, "this is John. John, Arsenio." The kid came over, folded his arm in front and bowed to me! Then he straightened up and held out his hand.

"Very pleased to meet you."

I didn't know what to do so I shook it. It seemed stupid. He turned to Jake.

"I did as you suggested," he said. "The salt is nearly gone, but the spot, I think, is out."

"John here is the one who showed me that trick."

"Then it is you I should thank," he said to me. "I'm always excited to find new ways to clean up."

Not only did he look funny, but he talked funny too. There was something else. Something that made me think I'd seen him before, or could have.

"Arsenio is half of the double two," Jake said. "Judith's the other. Where is she hiding out?"

"I put her in the closet," Arsenio said. "The one with all the old clothes and paper and crayons."

Jake nodded and puffed on his pipe. "Why don't you introduce John to her?"

Arsenio made a face, the kind that if I'd made I would have got a whipping. He didn't budge.

"Go on," Jake said.

"I don't want to."

"I can see that, but you must. She's undoubtedly already made a big mess."

"Do I have to?"

Jake frowned, as if the question didn't make any sense at all. He puffed on his pipe then lay back on the pillows and stared off into space. Arsenio sighed, then turned around and started off.

"Come on," he said.

I followed him out of the room into a hall with doors. Partway down I saw the pile of salt and made sure I didn't step in it. He stopped at one of the doors and straightened his bowtie. He smoothed down his hair with his hands. He was stalling, and I felt sorry for him.

"I live down the hall," I said.

He nodded. "Me too."

"Apartment 206. With my Mom and Dad."

"I live down *that* hall," he said, pointing to the one we had just walked down.

"You mean here? You live here with Jake?"

He nodded. "So does Judith. We live here together."

"Is she your sister?"

"She's my double. She lives on the other side."

"Which one is your room?"

He pointed to the orange one, which surprised me. I was about to ask him where his bed was, when all of a sudden there was a scream from the closet. It was loud and scary. Arsenio threw the door back and jumped inside. I took a step in, and stopped. The place was a mess. In back, under a pile of clothes was a girl. She had long hair that was all tangled, and her face was dirty. It was also red. That was because she was screaming.

"My foot, it's stuck, it hurts. It hurts!"

Arsenio didn't waste a minute. He jumped through the boxes and clothes and crumpled up papers, found where her foot was stuck and pulled it out. Then he straightened up and fixed his bowtie.

"Judith," he said, "you're a mess."

"So what?" she answered. She tore up a bunch of paper and threw it in the air. While it floated down, she wiggled around like a worm. Then she started on the clothes.

She was already wearing a dress, and she put pants on top of it and then a shirt and then another shirt and then a vest. She found some socks, all different colors, and put those on too. A hat, and then shoes. There was a mirror on the inside of the door and she looked at herself and smiled. Then she looked at me.

"Hi," she said.

"Hi."

"My name's Judith."

"Mine's Johnny."

"Want a sock?"

She gave me a red one, then a green one. Then she handed me her hat. Before I knew it, she was pulling clothes off as fast as she had put them on. They flew into the hall, and as fast as they landed, Arsenio picked them up and folded them. She got down to her undies and took those off too. Then she jumped up and ran down the hall, squealing.

"Oh no," Arsenio said. "We've got to catch her." He ran after her and I ran too. He caught her, but she slipped away. He started after her again, but stopped when he got to the orange room.

"Too late," he groaned.

Judith was already across the room. She was jumping up and down on the pillows, laughing and giggling with Jake. He was having fun too, and I wondered why Arsenio was so glum.

"Fun now," he said, "but he can only take it for awhile. Then we have to go back."

I shrugged, and wandered over. Pretty soon the three of us were rolling in the pillows, having a great time. But in a little while Jake's breathing got hard. He stopped playing, and then he told me and Judith to stop too. Neither of us wanted to, and Judith kept bouncing, which made me do it too. Jake said stop again, not loud but so you knew he meant it. He told Judith it was time for her to go.

"No no no," she begged. "Please don't make me."

"We just got here," Arsenio said.

"Please," I joined in. "Can't we stay a little longer?" He looked at each of us, and then he sighed. It was three against one. When he looked back, his eyes were twinkling.

"All right," he said. "A little longer. Time enough for a game of dominoes."

We all cheered, even though I didn't know what that meant. Jake told Arsenio to fetch the dominoes. Arsenio went to the table

with the blue box on it, the one that flashed on and off and rattled
when you shook it. He picked it up with both hands and brought
it over. This time it reminded me of waves of water when the sun
hits. I still couldn't see a lid.

From somewhere behind his back Jake brought out a cup of
water. At first I thought he was thirsty but he didn't drink it. Instead, he lifted it up in the air, turned it over and poured it on top
of the box. That seemed like a silly thing to do because he'd just
have to clean up the mess. But when I looked there wasn't any
mess.

Instead of spilling on the floor, the water fell right into the
top of the box. Into the wavy blue light. Suddenly, a tower of
spray shot out, like steam from a tea kettle, only cool. It misted
the air, making it hard to see. I had to wipe my eyes, and when I
looked again, the box was open. It was a great trick. I wanted to
ask Jake how he did it, but Judith and Arsenio had already
started taking the things out. The dominoes.

I'd never seen one before. They were all white except for the
dots on top which where were black. Some of them had a lot of
dots and some had only a few. Judith and Arsenio took them all
out and put them together with the dots facing up. Already it
looked like a fun game, and I waited to see what was next.

"We all get to choose a game," said Jake. "One game each, and
then everyone goes home."

Judith was the first to shout out. "Trains!" Right away she and
Arsenio started picking up the dominoes and lining them up on
their edges, one in front of the other. By the time I joined in they
had already used up most of the pieces. Judith ended up with the
longest line and I had the shortest. Mine wasn't so straight either,
it kind of curved, but no one said anything.

"You go first," Judith told me.

"Okay," I said, and I sat there, waiting for something to
happen.

"Go on," she said, "push it."

"Huh?"

"Like this . . ." She touched the domino at the end of her line, tilting it forward and making it hit against the one in front of it. That one fell down and hit the next one, and then all of a sudden, faster than I could see, the whole line fell down. Judith let out a whoop and Arsenio laughed. I just stared. It seemed like magic.

Arsenio did the same thing with his and it happened just like before. This time we all laughed. Then I pushed mine and the line went down like theirs, only in a curve. I loved the way it fell and especially I loved the clacking sound when it did. We all clapped, Jake too, and then Arsenio said,

"Now it's my game."

He took the dominoes out of the piles and started putting one on top of the other. Soon he had a tower that was almost as big as he was. He tried one more on the very top but it was too many. The tower fell over with a crash.

Judith built hers, but before it got too tall she stopped. She built another right next to it. When the second one was as tall as the first, she sat back. The corners of her mouth curled up, and I got ready for something. Quick as a mouse her hand jerked out, knocking the bottom dominoes out. For a second the towers leaned, and then the whole thing came crashing down. I laughed. Then it was my turn.

I built three towers next to each other, and when I was done, I looked for something to balance on top. Something special. The first thing I thought of was the black box.

It was back on the table, looking even blacker than before. It seemed to suck at me, and I couldn't keep still. I went to it. I was afraid to touch it, afraid not to. I reached out. Then Jake began to whistle.

It was a low, cold sound, like the wind in winter. I stopped and listened. He cupped his hands in front of his mouth, and the sound changed. It got higher, prettier, like sometimes you hear in the park. It filled the room, and then he separated his hands. In his palm was a tiny blue bird. Its beak was open, and it was singing.

Jake held it to his lips and blew on it. The bird flew into the air. It circled the room, singing its pretty song, then landed on my towers. Its tiny beak opened, and it sang its song to me. It turned to Arsenio, then to Judith, singing to each of them. Last of all it turned to Jake.

It sang to him, and Jake sang the same song back. Then he opened his mouth. The bird leaped into the air, flew once more around the room, then dove between Jake's lips. That scared me, but nothing happened. The bird just disappeared. Jake closed his mouth, and then we all started clapping.

"No need for that," he said. "It's really not difficult. And now it's time for John's game."

They all looked at me and I looked down in my lap. I shrugged.

"Make one up," Judith said.

"Yeah," said Arsenio.

I shook my head. "You."

The two of them looked at Jake.

"Fine," he said. "I'll be the last. We'll play the matching game."

"Matches?" I said, thinking of the long, skinny one he lit with his fingers. He hushed me.

"Listen, and I'll tell you.

"Each domino has one or more than one dot on it, except for the one that has no dots. That one is called the double blank, and also it's called the soul. Every other one has a name too. There are twenty-eight in all, and every person in the world has one that is special to him. After the soul comes the sun, the one that has a blank on one side of the black line and one dot on the other. It's called the moon too sometimes, and the eye. After that comes the double one, with one dot on each side of the line. Its name is moon eyes and snake eyes, and in some places it's called the scream. The next one has one dot on one side and two on the other, the funny man, or the cripple. Then there's the double two."

"That's ours," said Arsenio and Judith.

"The twin," Jake nodded. "The mirror. The dots go all the way up to six; the domino with the most dots has six on one side and six on the other, twelve in all. It's called double six, tracks, the journey, and sometimes it's called grief."

I looked at the dominoes, trying to get what he was talking about. But after awhile, all the dots started floating and mixing together. I had to blink to make them stop. I liked hearing the names and stuff, but building the tower was more fun. I didn't want to hurt Jake's feelings but I told him anyway.

"More fun now," he said. "But I have to think of the future. I'm the one who has to think of that."

He lined up the dominoes in a different way, so that the dots were matched up.

"You don't have to remember the names," he said. "All we're going to do is match them. Like this."

He put the soul in the middle of the floor and on one end he put the one with a blank and one dot and on the other end he put the one with a blank and two dots.

"Judith's turn now."

She snatched up her own special domino, the twin, and matched it with the one on the floor. Then Arsenio picked up one with two dots on one side and six dots on the other.

"What's this called?"

"The goof," Jake said. "Slippery luck."

"Goof," repeated Arsenio, and matched it to the domino on the floor.

I looked around for a good one and spotted the one with six dots on one side and nothing on the other. I picked it up.

"Tracks through snow," said Jake. "Soul in ice. Home."

I matched it with the other one with six dots. Then Jake put one next to it, then Judith, and pretty soon all the dominoes were laid out in a line. It looked neat, like a long snake with spots. Then Judith messed it up. I gave her a look, and so did Arsenio. Then I looked at Jake.

"Again," I said.

He smiled. "Of course. Another time. Now it's time to put them away."

None of us liked that but we didn't argue. We helped put the dominoes back in the box. When they were all in, the top turned blue, like before. Then it started flashing.

"Now it's time to go home," Jake said.

I know two different ways to be sad. One is when someone hurts you, or you're afraid they might. The other is when you're having fun and it has to stop. I was sad the second way, which is better than the first. I knew there'd be fun again.

I said goodbye to everyone and walked to the front door. Just as I got there I remembered something I forgot to say, and I turned back. But when I got to the edge of the room I stopped. Jake and Arsenio and Judith were in the middle of something that looked important. It looked private too, and I didn't want to butt in. But I didn't want to leave either. I couldn't.

Arsenio and Judith were standing in the middle of the room with their backs touching. Their eyes were closed, and Jake was whispering to them. He bent down and kissed them on their heads. Then he went to the table with the black box on it. He did something which I couldn't see, then stepped back. The box was open. In his hand was a domino. The twin.

It was white, and bright as a cloud. So bright that I had to squint to see it. He held it above Judith and Arsenio, then took his hand away. By some trick the domino stayed. It hung in the air, shining like a cloud, floating. Slowly, it began to turn.

Each time the domino turned, Judith and Arsenio got smaller. I don't know how, but little by little they shrunk until they weren't much bigger than mice. And they kept shrinking, until they were as tiny as bugs.

Then Jake took the domino and put it on the floor next to them. They walked apart, and each grabbed an edge. Pulling hard, they climbed on top. One of them stood on one side of the line, the other on the other. The domino got brighter. And brighter still. Finally it got so bright I had to look away. There was a flash, and when I looked back, they were gone.

Jake put the domino back in the box, and I decided it wasn't so important after all what I was going to say. I turned around and tiptoed away. When I got to the door, I ran as fast as I could home.

I wasn't so lucky when I got there. Mom and Dad weren't in the bedroom anymore. They yelled at me and asked where I'd been. I said on the stairs, and they told me not to lie. Then Dad took off his belt.

I tried not to cry because that just makes it worse. Instead, I thought of Jake and his dominoes, of Arsenio and Judith and the box. And thinking of them made the whipping not so bad. The hurt seemed farther away.

Things changed for awhile after that. Dad lost his job, and Mom got laid off for a few weeks. Everyone was home alot, which was actually pretty nice. Dad fixed the TV, and Mom cooked and talked about what a nice family we were. Sometimes she worried about money, but that would make Dad leave. He'd come back with beer, and they'd make up. Then they'd get drunk together.

I watched TV and played a lot with GI Joe and the other guys, except that I gave them new names, like Jake and Judith and Snake Eyes and Cripple. It was fun being home. Everyone was happy. Then there was a fight.

It started out small, and Dad left. I thought he was going for beer, but he didn't come back for a long time. Mom got madder and madder. I turned off the TV and put away my toys. I stayed as quiet as I could.

Finally, he came home, as drunk as I'd ever seen him. The two of them yelled at each other, then Mom took off her shoe and threw it. Dad just laughed, and she threw the other one. That one hit him in the face, and he stopped laughing. He took off his belt.

Then Mom was the one who laughed. She said he was too drunk to do anything, but she was wrong. He slapped her across the neck. She tried to grab the belt but he yanked it back and slapped her again. She screamed, and I got scared. I begged them to stop.

"Go to your room," they said, but I couldn't. I just stood there, while they kept on fighting. It was awful, worse than ever, and I almost started crying. But crying was the last thing I wanted to do, so I did what they said. I went to my room. Only I never made it inside.

When I got to my door, something happened. I don't know what, but suddenly everything changed, like when a noise you've been listening to for so long you've forgotten about it suddenly stops. Like that I stopped hearing my Mom and Dad. Everything got as quiet as could be, and then, real soft, I heard the Ant Song. It was up to four.

"The ants go marching four by four, hurrah, hurrah. The ants go marching four by four, the little one marches out the door, and they all go marching down, to the ground, to get out of the rain, Boom, Boom, Boom . . ." And I walked to the front door and marched out.

Jake's door was open, and I went in. He was lying on the pillows smoking his pipe, blowing little clouds in the air. He smiled when he saw me and waved me over. In his lap was the cat, the black and white one with the long fur. He was petting it, and the cat was purring.

"Sit down," he said, and I did. All of a sudden I started to cry.

The tears busted out like rain and I tried to stop, but that only made me cry harder. Jake wiped my nose with a hankie. He said that the tear lakes had to get dried up, which wasn't easy. It was spring, and all the snow up above was melting. I guess he knew what he was talking about because it did take a long time. But finally the lakes dried. My throat and chest were sore, but I felt better. The first thing I wanted to know was where were Judith and Arsenio.

"Home," he said.

"Can I go there?"

He puffed on his pipe and looked at me. "There's always room."

"I want to go."

"Patience, my boy. There are many homes, you know."

"I want to see Judith and Arsenio."

"There are others. Hundreds. Thousands. Lost children, sad children, crippled and sickly children. From any war you choose. Any famine, any plague. From Sumer, Saxony, Bombay, Peru. Any place. Any age."

"Huh?" ·

"Each person has a stone, John."

"A stone?"

"A domino. One that is his own. I told you that before."

"I want to see."

"You shall. If you're going to live here, you need a place."

He pushed himself slowly to his feet. The cat hung on to him as long as it could, then scrambled to the floor. Jake went across the room and got the black box, brought it back and sat down. He said some words which I didn't understand. He said them again, and the black hole that was the box got even blacker. Like it was swallowing itself with more and more blackness. There was a hiss, and suddenly it was open. Inside were the dominoes.

On top was a long row, all of them matchers, starting with the soul and ending with the tracks. They were white as snow when it's falling, before the ground makes it dirty. White as new teeth. The dots were like coal. One by one Jake took the dominoes out and laid them on the floor.

"Now you must choose," he said.

"Huh?"

"Pick one."

Well that was easy. I knew which one I wanted, and I reached for the twin. But when I picked it up, I saw that it wasn't the twin at all. It was the one with six dots on one side and nothing on the other.

"Big ice," Jake said. "The palace."

"I don't want this one," I told him. "I want the other."

"Indeed." His eyebrows came down and he gave me a sideways look.

"I want the twin." I pointed to it. "That one."

He rubbed his chin. "Hmm," he mumbled, playing with his hair. Finally, he took the domino out of my hand and put it back on the floor. Then he mixed them all up.

"Pick the one you want," he said. "Last chance."

Before they made me dizzy like before, I found the one I wanted. I said to myself, okay this is it, and took a deep breath. Then I reached down and picked it up.

It was the same one as before. The six and the blank. That got me scared. I glanced at Jake, who didn't seem to be looking, and tried to put it back. Only it didn't go back. It kept sticking to my hand. I didn't know what was happening, if it was magic or what, but I didn't like it. I felt like crying again.

"Help me," I said.

Jake looked up and smiled. He took the domino out of my hand. With his fingers he touched each dot, then he nodded.

"It's yours, John."

I shook my head. "I don't want it."

"Nevertheless . . ."

"I want to go home."

"Of course."

I got up and started moving my legs, only instead of going forward, I stayed in the same place. When I looked around, it seemed like the room was getting bigger. The chairs, the tables, the pillows were all growing. The dominoes too. Instead of being flat on the floor they had turned into little boxes, then big boxes, then bigger ones. And high above me, something was twirling in the air.

It sparkled like a mirror in the sun, sending light down on my body. I wondered what it was, then suddenly something grabbed it from the air and put it on the floor next to me. Then I knew.

It was as big as the other dominoes, and I remembered what had happened to Arsenio and Judith. I had become tiny like them, but I didn't feel scared. Just the opposite, I felt brave and ready for an adventure.

I grabbed the edge of the domino, pulled hard with my arms and kicked with my legs. I scrambled on top, then nearly fell in one of the holes. It looked safer on the other side, but to get there I had to jump over the line in the middle. I nearly fell in that too. Then the domino started to glow.

It got brighter and brighter, so bright that I had to cover my eyes. There was a flash, and then the brightness was gone. I opened my eyes, expecting to see Jake or the cat, or even my Mom and Dad. But what I saw was a big field of snow, and faraway, a building. There were footprints in the snow and lots of kids, but I'm not supposed to tell even that much. If you lived in the dominoes, I could, but then I wouldn't have to because you'd know. And anyway, everybody has his own domino. That's what Jake says. It means that everybody already knows, or they could. And I like that because then I don't have to tell. No matter what I don't have to.

DROWN YOURSELF

Johnny Jukes knew the woman was an android. She stood on the edge of the dancefloor, outside the ring of frenzy, cool and detached. She had sandy hair, almost blond but not, cut severe. On one side it hung straight, clipping the part where her neck turned into shoulder, half covering her eye. On the other side it was cut off high, nearly to the ridge of her skull. On that side her scalp was visible, the ripples of skin, the tiny blue veins. She had outlined the veins with a tattoo. It looked like a water course from a thousand miles up. Water music. The band riffed junk and screwed it in.

With an unerring eye Johnny Jukes knew she was not human. She stood on the wall, hugging a corner. Her eyes were flat, staring into the heaving crowd without a flicker. Long fingers of one hand wrapped around the base of a brown bottle, which she held at her side. When she put it to her lips and poured it in her mouth, it was like adding oil to a car. Her eyes didn't move and she didn't swallow. When she was done, she wiped her mouth with the back of her hand. Her lips were blue, like the veins on her scalp.

Nursing a bottle from a half-floor above, Johnny Jukes stared at her and knew. She was all edges. She stood erect on the wall, like the scabbard of a sword. She did not slouch. Her clothes were crisp, like whole numbers. They were dark, except for her boots, which were red. Thorn of love. A screeching solo tore off a dozen dancers' heads.

Johnny Jukes stared and he knew. He knew that he had to have her. She was the most beautiful woman he had ever seen.

The scene was like this. Johnny Jukes, young man, fair-skinned, beardless, sat alone at a table at the Deaf Club. Drank a bottle for appearances. Smoked, if he had to, for appearances. Had never laid or been. Had never cared, until this night.

He had heard love drops like this. Like music, sudden, like a hand squeezing the heart. No past, no choice, just the hand squeezing until you give in. You get no breath, no rest until you give in. Like if you see Noah and the Safe Ark, and beneath them you see the roiling, angry, fathomless sea, you give in and choose the sea. You drown yourself in the sea. That's love.

Johnny Jukes pushed his chair back and stood up. He threw the last fingers of juice down his throat in mimicry of burly biker men. He adjusted his leather jacket, zipped it up then changed his mind and left it half-open. He took shades out of a shoulder pocket and slipped them on. He could see enough. If he got it down right, the people would move out of his way.

At his back was the second level bar. There was one above and another on the floor below. All three were packed, sucking people to them like black holes. The sweet sick smell of metabolized alcohol poured from mouths, mixed in the air with dense smoke. Beneath ran the swollen hope of drugs, their odor oozing steadily from sweat pores. People shouted at close range while rubbing against bodies on all sides. Some sucked face with wide open mouths an inch apart and thick, fleshy tongues. Nobody noticed Tough Johnny Jukes.

He pushed and apologized his way through the crowd. When a space opened, even a knife thin one, made maybe by two people blowing out their breath at the same time, he jumped in. He did it sideways, using his shoulder, and then he waited until the crowd shook itself down and the next opening appeared. In this way he reached the stairs.

He could not see the stairs. They lay under a dense grapple of body parts. Bodies launched themselves on top and were either carried or thrown off. A person in a scarlet wet suit landed near Johnny Jukes' feet, rolled himself up clutching his side, grinning in pain and relief. Johnny adjusted his leathers and leaped. He was young and sure as fire. The human insect groaned; its probing fingers pushed him down. He landed on the floor on his back, got up quick before someone went down on him. He scanned, looking for the lady. She had not moved. He played with his zip, close enough now to be afraid. Tough Johnny, aka Callowman, Yutemon, The Great Pretender played with himself on the verge of his truth. It was stark: the boy had never had it before, never, not on two or three or four, not with a stick or a gauge, plasmatics, actifiers or selectics. He was as clean as outer space.

The bassman hit subsonics, loosening sphincters and jamming circuits in the Deaf Club.

Johnny Jukes adjusted himself and moved out, an acre of desire sucking at his chest like a magnet. He collided with homespun, acne-pocked boys and girls, masks concealing executive luncheons and biscuit-laden dead breakfast tables. He trampled through the mob, uninterested, but the fight jacked him up. His manners had been learned at the Club, from the solo table. The boy girl scene he snatched with eyes and ears. Violence was a stimulant drag.

He got to the woman on the wall, swaggered whole body an inch from her face.

"One plus one equals one," he said.

She drew her serpentine eyes from their drapery apartment. "Get out of my face, Jack."

"Johnny Jukes," he said. "We meet. Give it your attention."

"The meter's stuck, Jack. The terminal's down."

"Johnny Jukes," he repeated dumbly, stunned by her high melting point. "It's a crave. Flat out."

Her chest heaved (could there be sorrow at the Deaf Club?).

Blue lip corners inched up. "It's no lock, Jack. Can you raise the dead?"

Jukes smiled. He felt brittle as paper and twice as big. Since she wasn't inclined to turn her head, he backed straight off, tamping the crowd behind him. He drew down the zipper of his jacket, and when she indulged him with a smile, he unzipped it all the way. The two sides of leather drifted apart, revealing a chest and belly as smooth as ice. On the platform above, the band cut head. Fire raged, and beasts flew from amps. Johnny Jukes began to dance.

He was swift but not agile, clean but without grace. He kept his angles sharp and his rhythm carefully idiosyncratic. The girl watched, impressed and amused. She had a feeling about this kid, but her senses were melted by the bottle and the derms on her skin. She couldn't quite shake it down. She relaxed and let the scene play itself. The Deaf Club was where she made life easy.

Johnny Jukes kept moving, spasms and crude geometry. His head jerked, and his shades flew off. He crushed them under heel, making the woman laugh. She emptied her bottle and dropped it to the floor, kicking it to him with the spike of her boot. He snapped the neck easily with a toe and ground the glass into the floor. He looked up hopefully, and she was smiling. He danced on.

What went through his mind was this. Bright flapping birds, the tails of fish thrashing on the bottom of boats. An arc welder, fusing metal. He was wrapped in the skittish heat of himself. In the deaf, incautious lie of passion. He would expose himself for virgin love and a handful of flesh. Pull down the pillars of the temple for the taste of this woman. For her flesh. And the crimson sea asked, the blotting randy sea, what flesh? After all, she was an android.

Johnny Jukes got very calm then. He got curious. How would they go about it? Would she warm up to him? Could she? He knew nothing about sex and he feared fumbling. Would it matter? What did it take to satisfy an android?

He went over to her, hanging in her face, sucking up the scent. Drugs was in her, and quick little molecules of sexual excitement. Her nostrils dilated when she breathed.

"You fixed me?" Johnny asked formally.

"Yeah," she said, moving her empty hand, touching his chest with a finger. "I spelt it."

Johnny grinned like an idiot, exploding sensations causing momentary paralysis. He wanted to grab her but couldn't make the right connection. He opened his mouth and stuck out his tongue like he had seen the other people do. She gave him a narrow look and took back her hand. She remembered something.

"Swallow it, Jack," she said coolly.

He closed up at the command and searched her face nervously. "It's Johnny Jukes," he said in retreat.

"Yeah," she said, softening a bit. "I don't take people in the face, Jukes."

"I'm sorry," he said, regretting having to say it. But she didn't seem to mind. With a finger she traced the blue lines on the bare side of her head.

"This scene has a past," she said thoughtfully.

"It's a first," Johnny protested.

"What it is," she replied, going inside, considering the game. It had happened like this once before, she was sure. He had made her on the floor and they had gone to the can for the rest. But she couldn't remember the rest, and had a feeling that maybe there wasn't. A taste of danger intrigued her. She made up her mind.

"It's operational," she said, turning away. "Count it down."

She pushed her way through the crowd at the bar on that floor, climbed on a guy's back and threw some coin on the counter. She reached over and grabbed a couple of open bottles, then slid to the floor, using her hip to get back out. Johnny followed her to an empty table in the back.

"You take baths, Jukes?" she asked, after halving the beer in a swallow. He shook his head.

"Me neither. I got this theory that we're all going to drown someday. After we burn up here. We started in water and we end there. It's a sensible thing."

In the other room the band cranked seven nine, and the bottles rattled on the table. I'm already drowning, thought Johnny.

"You're the most beautiful person I've ever seen," he told her.

She laughed and dropped back in her chair. "Back to business, huh Jukes?"

"I can't get you out of my mind. From the moment I saw you."

"Lust is a happening thing."

He shook his head. "It's love."

She raised her eyebrows. "Let's jack it up then."

From a boot she slid out a wing of plastic with tiny colored panes pasted on. She peeled one off and stuck it in her mouth against a gum. She got another and offered it to Johnny on the tip of her finger. He took it and copied her.

"I got a theory about love," she said, as her body began to rush away from her like a river. She grabbed her breasts to keep the nipples from exploding. "It comes in packages. Like candy. Except there're no labels, so when you go to the store you never know what you're getting. They make it in a big warehouse under the sea. Package it in the dark. It has to be dark, because light destroys it. Light is like a deathray to love. You follow, Jukes?"

"I have to have you," he said. "I've never felt like this before."

"Last night, Johnny boy. Except then you had the shades. I couldn't see your eyes."

"No," he said, hurt and confused. "I'm not that kind."

"Everybody's that kind," she said, finishing the bottle. "If they get boosted enough." She looked at him.

"What if I say I don't do it, Jukes? I don't split the seam for Jacks and Janes."

"I understand," he said quietly. Then he turned fervent. "It doesn't matter. Really. I don't care what you are."

She gave him a look, then laughed. "You got me sussed, eh Jukes? You scan me far off, suss me with your hand on the trigger. You conjure it in your head and think that's all there is." She leaned across the table, grabbed him viciously by the leather. "I told you, Jack, it's no lock. The goods are in the ocean and it's deep. You know how deep an ocean can be?"

Johnny nodded into her face with frightened eyes. He felt innocent and way over his head. She saw this and loosened her grip. She slumped back.

"Forgive," she said. "It's all such a drag." Then she smiled and touched his face with a finger. "You're sweet. Put up with me for another drink, and we'll make a run."

He nodded dumbly and offered her his untouched bottle. Maybe he could get back on track. She downed the juice, then got out of her chair and strode to the dark hall at the end of the room. Her gait was remarkably steady. Johnny Jukes followed like a baby duck, his program starting to swell with intimations of manhood.

The short hall was broken by three doors, none of them marked. Along the wall opposite them fidgeted the divers who needed their quick fix in private. They were a sorry lot, bug-eyed and clammy faced. Twitchy twitchy. Interspersed were the ones who forgot to take the pills, the anti-diuretic ones the management dispensed at the door to keep the clientele from pissing. A bloated trans who couldn't wait dropped his skirt and unloaded in a corner.

Johnny Jukes' dream machine came on the scene like a shark in shallow water. She knocked once on a door, waited five seconds, then slammed it hard with the flat of her forearm. The flimsy slide bolt splintered off and the door flew open. In another five seconds she was dragging out a red-faced skinhead, his pants at his knees.

"Jerking off," she said disgustedly, pulling starstruck Johnny in by the lapels. She slammed the door closed and wedged it tight with the doorstop. As added precaution she jammed the trash can between the edge of the sink and the doorknob. Then she turned to her man.

"Well," she said, her body starting to fill the room. "Well well well."

Johnny stared at her hungrily. He wasn't sure what to do. He felt like ripping her clothes off but was afraid it might make her mad. He had never been this far before. Overheard phrases from the boys at the Club didn't help. He was dazed, and his body was turning to stone.

Not so the lady. The quick action had jacked her up, and she wanted more. Her head was miles out and her body felt like the mantle of a youthful planet. She sauntered to the object of her desire and tore off his jacket. With quivering fingertips she traced his skin from neck to navel. It was as bare as bone.

When her hand touched his belly, Jukes grabbed it by the wrist, nearly cracking the joint. Through pain the woman smiled, reassured by her power. She shook him loose, not easily, and went for the strings at the front of his pants. He slapped her down, once, twice, three times. He came alive.

He lifted her by the elbows and put her on the sink. On the wall behind was a shattered mirror, and above it a speaker with a wire running to the Club's PA. Unconcerned by pieces of himself in the mirror, Jukes went on tiptoe to the speaker. He twisted the knob to max, and suddenly the room got teeth. The band had gone to the gate of pestilence. The Deaf bassman was working harmony with capillary walls, making dots of blood appear on the skin. Higher up, a solo line had synched with nerve sheaths, causing muscles to twitch out of control. Johnny Jukes felt a savage thrill like the union of metals. He faced the lady, and with shaking fingers began to tear off her clothes.

She watched him, the intensity of his boyish face stirring her memory. When he took her heavy breasts in his hands, one in each, and in awe whispered, "they feel so real, so full of life," it came back. Through the derms, the panes, the bottles she remembered the night before. It struck her first as funny, and then a little sad. It worried her that she'd forget such a thing.

She pushed his hands away and got down from the sink. She

took a breath to speak, but Jukes was already on his knees pulling
at her pants. With a sudden give they popped over her hips and
dropped down to her ankles. He was panting, and she stood before him naked. Drops of perspiration wetted her pubic hair, and
an unmistakably human scent filled the air. Jukes stared, caught
in the lie.

The woman smiled at him, as kind a smile as she could manage. She touched him and gently got him to stand. Quickly,
before he could stop her, she untied his pants and pushed them
down. Where the legs met in front was smooth and hairless. It
looked like the inner crook of an elbow. Or, she thought, the sexless web between her fingers.

Johnny Jukes did not look down. Already in shock he turned
away from the body of the most beautiful woman he had ever
seen. His eyes caught the mirror, which reflected a hundred tiny
android parts, a hundred numbing truths. His mind tumbled in.
At that moment the band went simple, soft and simple. A single
line of ruthless penetration. It was first degree, jamming plenty,
dead stations and flashy dreams alike. Jukes blanked for sure.
Pinned by the music. Or by the blasts of crooked truth. Cause
and effect were hard to figure at the Deaf Club.

The woman sighed and played absently with herself, trying to
retrieve the scene. It was hopeless. The pane had worn and she
didn't figure another. The Jukes kid was static. Someone was fist-
ing the door.

She pulled up her pants and put on her shirt. When she was
done, she got his jacket from the floor and managed to get his
arms through the sleeves. All the time he was motionless, his face
stuck like a parachute halted in mid-air. She tied the pants and
zipped the coat, then stepped back one last time to piece the
boy. He was pathetic in his paralysis, almost lovable. She felt confused, angry, frightened by her own need. It was a scary thing to
think what she might have done for a machine.

"Light is a deathray to love," she said, listening to the words
decay. "Fix that, Jukes. Fix it tight."

She slapped down the trash can and kicked the door-stop, then pushed him out. A pale schoolboy rushed past and slammed the door. In the room the band had cranked it back. The party was lit, and heating. Johnny Jukes began to revive.

She found a table quick and got him in a seat. She wanted a bottle in his hand for the look, but when his eyes started to rove in unison, she took off. At the edge of the floor near the door she stopped and looked back. He was scanning the room with purpose, which made her shiver. She grabbed a bottle from someone's hand and tossed the juice down. Then she dove into the ant farm going out.

Johnny Jukes sat at the table, faintly lost but finding his way fast. The band was tight in his head. The circuits were lining up, and down deep the thorn of love was beginning to stir. He looked around. The kid had a feeling that this was going to be his night.

INTERVIEW WITH C.W.

C.W.'s house is almost impossible to find. It lies in the center of the city in a cul-de-sac connected to the crowded streets by the narrowest of alleys. It has no address and is surrounded by tall hedges, in one of which is a barely discernible pathway. Thorny blackberry bushes discourage passage, and poison oak is rife. Had I not received such a warm invitation I might have turned back rather quickly. But it is the first interview he has granted in nearly thirty years. It is unlikely he will live to grant another.

On this particular day the air is heavy with the promise of something. A culinary disaster, perhaps. Dark clouds in the shape of pots hang oddly near the peaked roof of his shingled house. Large birds, ravens possibly, congregate in the eaves. From old and rotted window boxes spill hundreds of bright flowers. I recognize helianthemum, alyssum, ranunculum and cistus, and there are other, more exotic types. On either side of the brick walk, which appears quite suddenly near the house, are large clay pots. Some are empty, while others seem to be the final resting place for broken and weathered statues. There is a flamingo, its long neck bent several times at right angles to each other. And a dancing bear, missing an ear and part of its nose. In one of the pots a single-winged angel balances on the nose of a seal, and from another juts a human torso whose head is nothing more than a steel reinforcement rod. As I approach the door I listen for sounds inside, but all I hear is the low and steady rumble of the city, broken occasionally by hoarse croaks from the black birds. There is no knocker on the door and I can't find a bell. After using my knuckles five or six times to no avail, I give up. Recalling that his invitation warned that he was a heavy sleeper, I search for other means to rouse C.W. Sticking out of one of the empty pots is a wooden baseball bat, on which has been carved, in lieu of Louisville Slugger or some such thing, "Exceptional Methods." The grip is comfortable, and once the bat is in my hands it seems clear what I am to do. Receiving no response to a final tap, I raise the bat and in one fluid swing knock down the door.

Behind it, to my surprise, is another. It is made of glass and opens quite easily with the knob. The hall in which I enter is dark and full of the smell of German cooking. In less than a minute C.W. himself greets me.

He has a lived-in odor to him, as well as another, more gamey smell. Red meat, perhaps. After shaking my hand, he steers me to a sitting room equally as dark as the hall. When he turns on a lamp, I get my first glimpse of him.

He is a short man, stocky and full in the stomach. He sports a full beard, which is dotted with breadcrumbs and hopelessly matted. His eyes are unreadable, lying as they do in the shadow of prominent brow ridges. Above them, almost in the center of his forehead is a depression, as though a part of his skull were missing.

He sits in a worn armchair and motions me to another near the lamp. I am careful as I walk because books are everywhere: not just on shelves and tables, but piled on the floor, even stuffed along the edges of the seat cushions. There is one at my back and a slimmer volume at my side. The first is The Aeneid, *in Latin. The other,* Jane Fonda's Workout Book. *Once I am settled, I turn on the tape recorder.*

CW (pointing to one of the books I've put on the floor): *Barbarella,* do you know it?

OB: I saw the movie, but it was years ago.

CW: The title has curious roots. Barb, Latin for beard, and ella, the Spanish female pronoun. A bearded lady. Quite possibly a hermaphrodite. Alternatively, it connotes a woman fond of using the razor. Delilah comes to mind. The movie, however, barely lives up to these promises. Barbarella, though impudent, is an unmenacing and largely pro forma sex attendant.

OB: This is an unusual house. How did you come to purchase it?
CW: The site was formerly a dioxin dump. The fear of death drove the price down, though not, perhaps, so much as the fear of mutation. I was destitute at the time, and my mood fit my resources. I've lived here for thirty years. Only one small tumor, which was rapidly excised.
OB: You talked about that in *The Shattered Man*. That was one gloomy book.
CW: You think so? As I recall, I felt quite light-hearted those months. Elated at times.
OB: The protaganist goes mad. A paranoid psychosis, if I'm not mistaken.
CW: After they removed the tumor, they put me on a drug to reduce brain swelling. It had curious effects on my mind. I ended up several weeks in a psychiatric hospital, part of which I spent working on the book. The first draft I finished in a week . . . I did not sleep the entire time. A week later, I burned the manuscript because it was so wretched. Also, I did not want it to fall into the wrong hands. It contained palindromic codes that might in certain quarters have set in motion unsavory events. In the final draft these were replaced by antipalindromes, designed to keep the cunning off balance. That there was little note given to the book's publication is evidence of my success.
OB: You've become quite a legend in the last few years, all sorts of exploits being attributable to you. Would you care to comment?
CW: Not especially. [He smiles]. You've travelled through thorns to a thorny man. Tell me what it is you want.
OB: I am thinking of some of the affairs you are purported to have had. Women have sued for paternity, men have accused you of being a carrier of disease.
CW: I have spawned two major literary movements. Collaborated on hundreds of plays and operas. Written essays, fiction, translations. And you ask about affairs?
OB: The sexual rites of the famous are talismen to the public.
CW: *Pubertal Buds*, yes? Don't I go on to say that sex fleeced of the

absurd is the product of the fascistic mind? And that fascism looks to sex and its brachiations as the tools of its power. Do you know what was here before the state made it a toxic dump? A whorehouse. Disposed of two birds with one stone. [He chuckles]. Now all they have to watch out for are gigantic, mutant whores.

OB: You have been dubbed by some a "language" writer. Could you explain what this means?

CW: It means various things to various people. To a poet it carries a structural, tectonic sense. To a prose writer, more a deliberate quality. To advertising executives it means damn good copy. My uncle Arthur used to say that words don't mean diddly squat. A curious phrase. He may well have been right. It's all a question of who's reading.

OB: Then you believe in challenging the reader.

CW: There was a song some years ago . . . by The Vandellas and Martha, I believe. "It doesn't matter what you wear, just as long as you are there . . ." It's the same with books. It's only a battle if you fight it. Unless, of course, you don't know how to read. Even then, as Pound used to say of Chinese characters, the words themselves have pictographic meanings. Our Arabic letters, for example, are perfectly styled for our current mode of living. Swift and clean, with a stab. The most telling cut is the not the deepest, but the smoothest.

OB: In *The Obvious Tear* you liken society to, alternatively, a hypodermic needle, a trip to the Vatican, and a particularly deep sleep. There is a side to your writing that many people regard as too bleak. They find it out of touch with reality as we know it.

CW: Don't you believe it. They eat it up.

OB: Your sales have dropped off considerably.

CW: Ridiculous. A man must write what he believes to be true. Or what he knows is false. The word must carry the power of commitment. Also, and take this as advice from one who has suffered thoroughly the unpleasant torment of dysphonia, it pays to enunciate. Depending on the inflection, the words "ma ma ma ma ma" in the Shan language of Burma mean either "help the horse" or "a mad dog is coming."

OB: I'm not surprised you use such an example. Deranged creatures have been a subtext through much of your work. The paranoid chimp in *The Risks of Evolution* and the rabid parrot in *Bristles at Home* come immediately to mind. I am reminded of Sir Adrian Bollocks' comment, "a man who looks to the animal kingdom for solace is a man who should have been born a rat." You seem to hold the opposite view.

CW: Do you have a vice? I think it is important for a man to have a vice. Preferably many, in which case it becomes a matter of consistent behavior. When we convince ourselves that we have but one, we run the risk of depression and self-abuse. It happens far too often that a man does not see and appreciate the organism he truly is. This inevitably leads to derangement, as you say. Whether it is a man or a mouse is hardly the point. When a writer writes about such a condition, presumably he is speaking from first-hand experience.

OB: I smell something burning. Is something on fire?

(C.W. pricks up his nose, then leaps out of the chair. As much of a leap, at any rate, that a man of his age and carriage is capable of making. He leaves and returns in a few minutes. His face is downcast but philosophic.)

CW: The meat is blackened beyond salvation. The pot is probably ruined. I suppose this is some message. I eat too much already, and yet I never care to stop. Where were we?

OB: Why have you not granted an interview for thirty years? And why break that silence to talk to me?

CW: Excellent, excellent. I've been very busy the last few decades. Metabolically speaking. Epistemology and work with the microscope have occupied much of my time. Facts must be digested. Eager ears spread disease, and prudence requires time.

As to you, there was something in your handwriting that gave me pause. The script was of a quality that suggested neuromotor compatibility. I was convinced that yours would be a sympathetic

mind. And you see? You broke down the door as you must, and yet did not criticize my cooking. My assessment was correct.

OB: It's been a great pleasure to meet you. I had planned to finish the interview today, but I seem to be falling asleep.

CW: A common reaction. It's all the words in the room. A source of great tedium, yet wonderful dreams.

I stagger from my chair, the tape recorder's microphone dangling near the floor. The air inside the room is no worse than that in the city, and yet I feel as though I've been drugged. I think C.W. leaves his chair to steady me, but I can't be sure. It may be that I manage the way out on my own. The door to exit seems made of leather; it is quite opaque. On either side of it are huge-leafed banana palms. I push, and in a moment stand once again in sunlight. The dark clouds that were present earlier have disappeared.

The path out is lovelier than the one in. It is lined with daisies, tulips and violets. Rhododendron blooms in the shade of dwarf maples and birch. A tiny brook gurgles in the distance.

I stop for a final look at the house. Its side is covered with dense ivy, and moss and lichen grow on the windows and their sills. A cat sits sunning on the roof, and in a hollow in the ivy sleeps a monkey and its mate. Strange indeed.

Eager to go to press, I turn from the house and push on.

SHED HIS GRACE

Four weeks before the beginning of the Olympics, when the torch was somewhere in the Great Basin of northern Nevada, a vast desert wilderness flowering perhaps after a late spring shower, T began to miss work. His supervisor, a benevolent woman with grown children, called him into her office one evening. A video monitor lay on her desk, its circuitry in disarray on the formica top. The severed wires of an old-fashioned microphone dangled over an edge. T stared uneasily at the desktop; he reached out to touch a damaged panel.

"Have a seat," she said. He stopped and looked up. She motioned him to a chair.

"Go on. Sit." He blinked and sat.

"You've been missing work lately. Is something the matter?"

He shook his head, staring at the dangling wires.

"You haven't been sick?"

He shook his head.

"You've got to let us know if you're not going to be here. At least call."

He looked up, blinking, then nodded.

"Maybe you need a couple of days off. You haven't taken a vacation in over a year."

He stared at the dead screen, anxious to have it working.

"Is it money? Is that it? Do you need some cash?" T saw his

reflection in the screen and looked quickly away. His supervisor took the sudden movement as a reply and smiled knowingly. She reached into the top drawer of her desk and took out some bills.

"Here. Pay me back when you get your next paycheck."

T took the money and stood up. His supervisor gave him a final look then bent over the desk and began fiddling with the inside of the monitor. T waited a few moments, then left the room.

He stayed that night for several hours after work, watching a new video from the neurosurgery department. He recognized the surgeon, even though most of his face was covered. The patient was awake during the operation, in a dissociated state of magnetically-induced euphoria. He conversed amiably with the operating staff, although from time to time — when certain parts of his brain were manipulated — his words made no apparent sense. At one point he repeated "jawbone" eighteen times in a row.

When the tape finished, T replaced the master in its file. He dropped a copy, which he had made while he watched, into his coat pocket. He locked the door behind him and left the hospital by way of its basement corridors, silent save for the rushing of waste through overhead pipes. Pushing through a heavy metal door to the street, he came into a night of fog and chill. The streetlights were barely visible; the hospital itself seemed wrapped in gauze. T turned the collar up on his coat and stuck his hands in his pockets. In one he found the bills his supervisor had given him. He had forgotten they were there.

He held them in his hand, frowning in concentration while he waited for a bus. Near the beginning of the video the patient had sung the opening bars of a song about money, but T could not remember the words. He had a tape at home of the President making a speech about economic policy, but all he could remember was Mr. Reagan's face. Thinking of it, T relaxed a little and put the money back in his pocket. When the bus came, instead of depositing a token in the machine, he gave the driver a handful of bills. He took a seat by himself, more confident now. His head was beginning to clear.

As the Olympic torch had made its way westward, carried by a young boy, a librarian, a man without legs in a wheelchair, T had secured his apartment. Now it was done, and as he entered he felt a certain resolution.

It was a single room, a studio with a small kitchenette at one end. A sliding glass door led the way to a narrow concrete porch which overlooked a back alley. T had covered the glass with a double layer of black velveteen, stapling it along the top edge and holding it snug against the floor with bricks. There were no other windows, and day in the apartment was as black as night.

Against the velveteen T had placed his monitors. Four rows of four each, sixteen in all, stacked in a square. On either side of this bank sat a video camera on a tripod; each camera was flanked by a pair of keylights. The hardware had been patched, and a single cable ran across the room to a panel on a table. Next to the table was a straightbacked wooden chair. In a corner of the room sat a cot. There was no other furniture present, and the single bulb in the ceiling had been removed.

T dropped his coat on the cot and went to the kitchen. He took a Coke from the fridge, popped it, and when he had swallowed half went and sat in the chair opposite the monitors. He lay his hand lightly on the keyboard at his side, his fingers settling into the familiar depressions of the keys. He pushed one and the dead screens sprang to life. Colored light filled the room.

He pushed a short sequence of buttons and in a moment the light was replaced by the image of a man running with a torch up the steps of a stadium. Tens of thousands surrounded him, and when he lit the Olympic flame, they cheered and sang. It was a tape of the beginning of the Games, and T began each of his days with it.

The opening ceremony ended and the face of the man was replaced by a boxing match, one of the day's events. A wiry Asian was stalking a black man; each was drenched with sweat. Blood welled from the black man's upper lip, and when the Asian punched his face, the blood flew into the air. The black man countered with an uppercut to the jaw, and the other man's head snapped back. Punches were thrown to the belly, one below the belt. T shuddered and hit a button. The boxers froze. T picked up a cassette that lay on the edge of the table and slipped it into the panel. The frozen images of the boxers stayed on the twelve peripheral screens, disappearing from the four center ones. In their place shone the face of the First Lady.

She wore a purple silk dress with a pink floral pattern across the bodice. The neck was high and ruffled, the sleeves short. Around a wrist she wore a gold bracelet.

She was in the midst of a tour of the White House, which T had recorded some months before. Her lips were red and smiling, her eyes bright. She made a demure gesture and turned down a long hall. The hem of the dress brushed against her calves, stroking them only inches above the mound of her heels. The scene shifted.

She was in a different room, standing under an elaborate chandelier. She was moving her lips, but T kept the audio off. She pointed to the chandelier, extending her arm with a ballerina's grace. The word FUCK flitted in the shadows of the loose skin of her arm as it entered the sleeve of her dress. T stopped the tape. He touched rewind, then magnification and play.

Mrs. Reagan's face took up the four screens, illuminated from above by a light source out of the picture. Bits of rouge and powder like crumbs of toast stuck to the pores of her skin. T increased the magnification as the camera swung down her cheek to her shoulder. Each thread of silk was visible, dark against the soft white folds of her axillary skin. T searched for the word in the shadows, stopping the tape, looking from screen to screen. It had gone, but he found other things hidden there. Grains of white powder covered the black tips of tiny hairs. A bead of sweat glistened on the loose skin. A drop of semen. A pale blue vein wound out of sight.

T studied the picture for hours. He found the thin surgical line where redundant folds of axillary tissue had been resected. Beneath the grains of powder he saw the roughage where a razor had excoriated the skin. Over and over his eyes searched the stubble of shaven hair. It seemed so certain. So simple.

T looked at the screens on the periphery, at the frozen shoulders of the boxers, rippling with muscles. He looked at the First Lady's armpit. The boxers. The armpit. He frowned and pushed a button.

Mrs. Reagan vanished as all sixteen screens came alive with boxing. The black man was bleeding more from his lip, and a new cut had been opened beneath his eye. He held up his hands to protect his face, and the Asian fighter struck him a series of blows to the midsection. One barely missed his genitals, and when he doubled over to protect himself, his opponent sent him staggering with an uppercut to the jaw. The black man fell against the ropes, and the camera held a close-up of blood running down his cheek. T grimaced and leaned forward in his chair. The shot changed.

A row of male swimmers crouched on blocks, arms thrown back. Their backs were taut and suddenly they uncoiled, arching out and over the water. They sliced through the pool like sharp tools, clean and strong. They flipped and turned with a mechanization that held T in awe. Finally they stopped, and the winner raised his hands in victory. He leapt from the pool, water dripping from his body, making the skin look like wax. T froze the shot and magnified it. The swimmer's chest was smooth, his legs and groin as barren of hair as a child's. The skin looked raw, as though it had recently been scraped by metal. His narrow suit was tight around his waist. It seemed to choke him.

T stared and cut the shot. He finished his Coke then stood from his chair and began to pace. The room was hot; he felt restless. Sweat began to build in his armpit, his crotch, and he removed his shirt and pants. The random light from the screens flickered on his body, casting a rough shadow on the opposite wall. T rubbed his chest and went to the kitchen for another Coke.

Sometime later he found himself in the shower, standing in a stream of cold water. He was shivering, and he stepped out to dry. He brought a stool in front of the sink and stood on it. The image of his chest reflected in the mirror on the medicine cabinet; the hairs were dark and curly. He rubbed them and opened the cabinet door.

The razor was new; he barely felt it. In the shower afterwards he felt as sleek as glass.

The next day his chest was sore, but the day after it was better. Each successive day he shaved it, and his legs, until the skin became accustomed to the razor. He rubbed oil into his pores, enchanted by the elegant smoothness of his skin. He did not return to work.

In the mornings, when the Games were not being televised, and often between events T watched tapes he had copied from ones at the hospital. Some were experiments on animals — cannulations of dogs, tumor induction in mice — but most were live surgeries on humans. A wide range of operations had been taped and grouped for study. The one marked *Plastic and Reconstructive Procedures* included a number of related operations: reduction and augmentation mammoplasty, resection of adipose tissue for morbid obesity, the use of the abdominal skin flap to reconstruct the penile shaft following accidental amputation. A green-masked surgeon was in the process of explaining the rationale for a certain lateral incision when his face dissolved into white noise. On each of the sixteen receivers a red light blinked, signalling the beginning of the Olympic telecast day. In a moment an announcer's face appeared. The after-image of the lateral pubic incision became his smile. His lips moved like the mouth of a fish, as T punched audio.

"Gold," the man was saying, "solid gold last night. The USA . . ." T cut him off. The voice was too jarring after the silent grace of the surgery.

The picture changed to a young man standing on a pedestal. His hands were clenched in a victory salute; above his head on a pole waved the American flag. The camera moved closer and

T recognized the face of the swimmer from before. His hair was no longer wet; T looked but could see no make-up. A sweatshirt covered his chest and around his neck hung a tri-colored ribbon with a gold medal attached to it. His eyes brimmed with tears.

T studied him for a long time before inserting the cassette of the First Lady. He pushed buttons to give her the center of the monitor bank, freezing the image of the joyful swimmer in a ring around her.

She was in an upstairs study beside a mahogany desk. One hand rested on the edge of the desk, which was smooth and polished so that it reflected light. In her other hand she held an open book, from which she was reading. The high collar of her dress fit snug around her throat. In the slack hollow of her jaw, in shadow, the word KNIFE was written. A blemish on the side of her chin was covered with flakes of powder. Her lips were carefully painted red; under magnification T noticed that the lipstick had begun to crack.

Mrs. Reagan finished reading the passage she had selected and replaced the book on its shelf. She pointed to a painting of a man flanked by an American flag. The man was a general, a president. She smiled and began to walk to the next room. T turned on the sound.

Her high heels clacked on the hardwood floor. The sound was a prodrome, a stimulant. She reached a tall door and pushed it open. Inside was a bedroom with a high-canopied bed that had not been slept in for years. The First Lady sat on the edge and began to discuss the history of quilt-making. T turned off the sound and watched her hands. Finely veined, powdered, she did not use them to speak. The gold bracelet around her wrist seemed too loose.

T stopped her and looked at the swimmer with the medal around his neck. His hands were clenched; Mrs. Reagan's were folded in her lap. Her lips were slightly parted; his were closed tight. T watched in fascination the tip of the first Lady's tongue. At length he pushed a button.

The two figures disappeared, replaced by a swarm of gymnasts. Young girls arched their bodies, split their legs on the floor, flipped in the air. T froze one upside down to examine the angle her legs made as they joined her torso. He brought the shot to medium magnification and followed the edge of her leotard across her thigh. He saw no hair, no sign of damage to the skin. He followed a lateral seam to her breasts, which were flattened by the extension of her arms. The outline of her ribs was visible through the tight suit.

T allowed her to complete the vault, watching her land and thrust her chest out like a bird. She skittered from the mat to the side of the arena, where she was hugged by a man and two other girls. All of them were blond. There were tears in the girl's eyes.

T reached for a cassette, stuck it in the recorder. The young girl's tears were replaced by the gloved hands of a surgeon. They had already completed an oblique abdominal incision and were in the process of mobilizing a section of colon. Deftly the fingers brought out a loop of intestine, placed two glass rods beneath it to prevent it from slipping back, then incised the front wall of the colon to provide drainage. The next section of the tape showed the technique for the placement of a permanent colostomy. The final part showed the care of the colostomy site, including attachment of the bag and disposal of fecal waste.

T stood and paced the room. It was increasingly hot, and the sweat that bathed his barren chest and axillae stung. The monitor screens were full of the noise between segments of tape.

T rubbed himself and looked down. His skin swarmed with thousands of rainbow spots. On the surface of his nylon shorts rose the shape of his genitals.

The screens came alive with the picture of a forceps and scalpel dissecting the necrotic edges of a burn. Bits of scab and dead tissue lay on a strip of gauze to the side. T turned away and went to the kitchen. The dark room lit up for a moment when he opened the refrigerator. He took out another Coke, squinting his eyes until the door closed, then drinking in darkness. When he was done, he crushed the can in his palm like he had seen someone do on television and threw it in the garbage. Then he went to the bathroom, took out his razor and shaved his head.

Mrs. Reagan was on her way downstairs, her hand sliding smoothly on the rail of the bannister. The camera angle from below made her seem tall. With each step the hem of the dress rode up her leg, exposing the edge of her shin and lower part of her knee. On close-up T saw the fine grains of make-up powder on the skin and beneath them, the narrow purple lines of her veins. The silky fabric of the dress stroked her as she came down the stairs.

At the bottom she paused, twirling the gold bracelet on her wrist. She turned a corner, walked partway down a long carpeted hall, then stopped with a finger to her lips. Her nail, red and glossy, glinted.

She pushed open a door, then stepped to the side. At the far end of the room, behind a large desk was her husband. He looked up and smiled. He was unperturbed by the interruption. He motioned her in.

T froze the picture as the President was in the process of standing. His head was bent forward and seemed about to fall on the desktop. On half the screens the Olympics returned. A two-hundred pound man was straining to press a one-thousand pound weight. His arms shook as he tried to lock his elbows. His face was bloated with blood. He raised the weight over his head, held it, then let it crash to the floor. The President's head was six inches from the desktop. The weightlifter staggered backwards, momentarily stunned. T froze the picture and magnified it. A blood vessel had burst in the lifter's eye, filling the white part with red. A thread of spittle hung from his lip.

T returned to the President and First Lady and pushed *Play*. Mr. Reagan raised his head and came around the desk to greet his wife. His smile was broad, his teeth capped in white. In the folds of skin at his throat animals rustled.

He made a benign gesture to the camera and reached out,

pulling Mrs. Reagan into view. They stood side by side, holding hands, chatting and smiling at each other. T noticed that Mrs. Reagan's bracelet had been pushed high up her forearm. It seemed to constrict the tissues beneath it, and the veins distal to it were engorged with blood. During the course of their conversation she loosened it, sliding it casually toward her wrist. In the crease it had left in the skin above, in faint relief, was the impression of a phallus.

T looked to the President, who seemed unaware of his wife beside him. He was jolly and strong. T pushed a button, and the frozen figure of the weightlifter was replaced by the same man standing on a platform draped with flags. He wore a sleeveless shirt, a jersey, and around his bull neck hung a gold medal.

T blanked the screens, all but the four at the top, which he froze. The President had raised his hand in salute, and his wife's face in profile was beaming.

He got out of his chair long enough to take off his shorts, then sat back down. He flipped a switch on the panel to his side, and the pair of keylights blazed on. They hurt his eyes, but he tried not to blink. He pressed a button, and the cameras warmed up. They were already focused on the spot where he sat, and in a moment the image of his chest and belly appeared on the bottom three rows of monitors. T moved a lever on the panel and the image on the screens shifted. It moved down to his crotch. His genitals.

He lifted his feet, which had been planted on the floor, up to the chair and put his heels together. This brought his pelvis out, highlighting his penis and scrotum. He moved slightly to one side, trying to eliminate shadow as much as possible. When he was satisfied, he got up and went to the kitchen.

He found a shallow pan and filled it with water, then lay it on one of the burners of the stove. After he had turned on the flame, he searched until he found a length of kitchen string, which he dropped in the water. He sharpened his stainless steel carving knife, then lay it beside the piece of string. He took another Coke from the fridge, swallowed it in three gulps, then went to the bath-room.

He lathered himself in the showerstall and shaved his groin and pubic area. Drying took less time now that he was hair-less. When he returned to the kitchen, the water in the pan was boiling.

He brought the pan and a pair of surgeon's gloves he had taken from the hospital into the other room and placed them at the foot of the chair. He positioned himself as he had before, keeping his eyes on the top row of screens. The President and First Lady gave him strength, and he pushed a series of buttons, extending them to the twelve screens on the periphery. On the four center ones were his genitals, pale and hairless in the bright light.

T stared at himself as he had at the swimmers. He reached down and rubbed until he was arched and strong. The glans bobbed gently to the sound of a silent anthem. Mrs. Reagan's gold bracelet dangled around her wrist. The President was smiling.

T leaned over and snapped on the surgeon's gloves. They were pale green, making his hands seem a part of someone else's body. He dipped his fingers in the water and took out the string, then settled back in the chair. He did not look at himself, watching instead his image on the screens. His penis was stiff, lady-like in its posture. His hands did not tremble as he grasped the ends of the string and wound them around the root of his penis and scrotal sac. He pulled the string tight and made a surgeon's knot, and another. The President smiled, the First Lady straight and certain at his side. For a second T lost concentration. His head turned giddy, he thought he heard a voice. The moment passed.

He stared at the screens. He was at the center, surrounded by Mr. and Mrs. Reagan. He leaned over and picked up the knife. Its edge glinted like gold in the light. Firmly squeezing the glans between thumb and forefinger, he began the amputation.

KEEPING HOUSE

I am here alone. Curtis left last week, was driven out, I should say. I have no regrets, except perhaps that I waited so long. If I am to preserve what we have, I need this detachment. I must be able to concentrate. Now more than ever I have to focus my will.

When I think how it all began, I want to laugh at our innocence. We were in the market for a house and were taken by our agent to a block where two were for sale, one next to the other. They had been built together at the turn of the century and were nearly identical. Each was two stories and shingled, with large bay windows facing east. The house to the north was in a poorer state of repair than the other, and when I queried various neighbors, I found that this had been the case for years. From what I gathered, its paint seemed to weather and its shingles to split faster than its twin, and the sidewalk in front always seemed to be cracked and filled with weeds. Curtis pointed out that it was by far the cheaper of the two, and whatever its deficiencies of structure or facade could easily be repaired for the difference in price. I reminded him that as an assistant professor of classics at the university I received a healthy stipend, and it seemed both unnecessary and absurd to suffer the inconvenience of renovation when the one next to it had been recently painted and was clean and ready for occupancy. Moreover, I was already experiencing antipathies, which, though vague, were sufficient to dissuade me.

Curtis remonstrated that I was making decisions based on super-
stition, an allegation I did not dignify with a reply. Shortly after,
we purchased the one I favored.

I believe now that neither of us was right, and we should have
avoided the neighborhood altogether. The house next door af-
fects other houses, ours perhaps most of all. Its walls abut ours, a
contact whose intimacy is impossible to escape. Like siamese
twins we share a circulation, the stealthy paths of mice and ants;
between us lies shelter for cockroaches and termites. I do not
imagine these things, for I have seen the severed paws and death
grins of mice caught in our traps. There are days when I have sat
for hours at my desk awaiting some invasion, other times when I
am certain that the steady drip I hear in the pipes is the prodro-
mal surge of a vile and infested sewage being directed at us from
next door. During the rains last year I began to notice thin and
shiny trails across the carpet in our daughter's room. One night
I rose to her crying, and upon entering her room touched with
my sole something fleshy and cold. My throat convulsed, and at
that moment I saw two beady eyes peering from within the bars
of her crib. Monstrous fantasies seized me as I slapped frantically
at the wall, searching for the light switch. When finally I found it
and threw back the night, I saw immediately how far my imagination had flown. My daughter was lying in her crib, already
back asleep. Next to her was a stuffed bear with radiant eyes, and
on the floor were two dark specks. I touched them, and recoiled.
Slugs. Trapped in the green fluid on my sole was the partial body
of another. Somehow I made it to the bathroom where, after
retching into the toilet, I disrobed and smothered myself in soap
and hot water.

For the next few weeks I dreamed about doing battle with
limbless creatures whose flesh dripped when punctured. I was
never vanquished, but neither was I ever victorious. The battles
were nightmarishly everlasting.

Curtis suggested that I act upon the source of these dreams,
meaning, as I understood, that I get rid of the slugs that infested

our daughter's room. I accepted the advice and plugged up a large space I found where the wall should have been snug against the flooring. It was a northern wall, and as I repaired it, I sensed that the crack would open again, that it was an entry being created by the pressure of the house next door. The fact that it was into Tanya's room, toward, that is, the most vulnerable member of our family occurred to me, but I quickly smothered the thought. Clearly, the dreams had upset me, and I tried to think with a mind like Curtis's, one that believes that nightmares can be stopped by plugging holes. My husband is as pragmatic as he is strong-willed. He is the kind of man a woman can trust when she can no longer trust herself.

Sometime in March we planted our garden, and when the lettuce broke through the ground a few weeks later, we began our nightly snail and slug raids. With flashlight and spade Curtis and I picked and crushed the slimy creatures. The task was never a delight, but as our slaughter climbed into the hundreds, my nausea abated. Shortly thereafter, the nightmares stopped.

In the middle of May Tanya entered her third year. Chirpy and ebullient, she was a bright and lovely child, testing limits, seeking forever to turn the world upside down. The garden flourished, despite weeds and thick blackberry brambles from the adjoining plot. I accepted a summer position with the university that provided childcare for Tanya and allowed me to escape the house. As June approached, I have to say I was as content as ever. Buoyed by new responsibilities away from home, by a daughter fighting and laughing down the corridors of childhood, by a husband who at last was beginning to find satisfaction at work, I became genuinely cheerful. I began to believe in myself and my power to overcome obstacles, and as a first step, I turned on the house next door.

At first I allowed it to remain, using my will simply to transform it to a thing of little consequence. When I passed the house in the morning, I blurred my eyes, imagining it to be less solid than a cloud, less real than a dream. I turned its roof into the feathered back of a small bird, its shingles into the bird's tufted belly. And when the wind blew, it was not so hard to pretend that the house had taken flight.

Later, I devised an even more powerful technique. I found a way in my mind to merge one wall of the house with another, eliminating perspective and the lessons of vision. Solid forms I deconstructed, melting their complex geometries into simpler dimensions. Little by little the house came to subtend but a single plane, composed of two intersecting lines. I fused the two into one, and then the one line into a single point. I wrestled with this point for nearly a week before, after a supreme effort, I caused it to disappear.

The house had gone. I had eliminated my chief foe. When I passed it now, I saw nothing, not even an absence. I felt finally safe from the waves that used to press me into panic and make me doubt my sanity. With relief I turned my mind homeward.

Despite our happiness that summer I knew that I had more to give. Freed from the preoccupation that had fed unnaturally within me, I vowed to show Curtis the love I knew I was capable of.

I began to pay more attention to our own house, cleaning it in the hours after work, trying to keep it tidy. I started a program of daily mopping of the kitchen and bathrooms, and every two or three days I vacuumed the rugs in the other rooms. The dirty dishes and glasses, which had always irritated me, now became constant reminders of failure. The demands of work, a child, married life and the new regime on which I had embarked kept me forever in the position of trying to catch up. I had to make a change, and after weeks of turmoil I made a decision: with money we had saved for our yearly vacation I went out and purchased a dishwasher. Certainly I regretted having to lose our vacation, but the disappointment was more than compensated for by my satisfaction and relief. The glasses were finally spotless, the counters clean, and I was once again in command.

After a few weeks of this routine I began to notice things

about the house that had never before occurred to me. For instance, even though we were adjoined on both north and south by other homes and thus had windows facing only east and west, the light in all the rooms sat distinctly on the southern walls. By this I do not mean the actual sunlight, which in the late fall and winter when the sun is to the south slants northward, but rather the radiance, the luminosity of the air. There seemed to be a glow, an enhancement, that hung upon the austral walls, and I could not account for it by any difference in the texture of the plaster or color of the paint. Conversely, the northern sides of the rooms seemed in perpetual penumbra, as though some substance around them were absorbing free light, trapping it, as it were, in shadow. This was manifest in morning as well as afternoon. With some consternation I discovered that it obtained even at night when the rooms were illumined artificially.

I removed the pictures and posters that hung on the darkened walls, transferring what I could to the south side of the rooms. For several days I mentally juggled the furniture, trying to rearrange it so that it lay beyond the border that shadowed the north. I finally settled on a position several feet from the wall, which placed it in an area of adequate illumination and seemed at the same time to preserve the symmetry of the room. Curtis expressed doubts as to the new arrangement but allowed to give it a try, reaffirming my feeling of self-confidence and trust in our relationship. I remember that a wave of gratitude passed through me, and I decided to do something special.

The next day after dropping Tanya at her daycare, I went shopping. I had in mind to buy a pair of slacks that Curtis had recently admired on a friend of ours. I found them in the window of a downtown store, and after the sales clerk had assured me that no one else had tried the pair on, I entered a booth and stepped into them. They were rose-colored and cut tight, clinging like another skin so that I had to suck in my breath to fasten them. At the mirror I was amazed at how they transformed me, as though the fabric were infused with a vitality of its own. The sales clerk coyly said nothing, though I am certain she must have known of their power. On the bus home I clutched the pants to my lap with a rising excitement.

I coaxed Tanya to bed early and made quick rounds of the house, tidying and cleaning up. Several pictures seemed slightly askew, and as I straightened them, I noticed that the windows needed washing. Resolving to do it the next day, I went to the bathroom and drew a bath. While it was running, I wrapped myself in a robe and rounded the bedroom, picking up the dustballs that had accumulated since morning.

Normally I do not like baths, but before the sexual act they seem appropriate. Somehow the touch of the water, its shapelessness and transparency, prepares me for what is to come. This time, however, the water seemed less than clean. I spied oily spots and strands of hair floating on the surface, and beneath them I sensed the pull of unsanitary currents. I began to feel that I was being covered by a coat of grime and quickly stood up, pulling the plug and watching to make sure the water drained fully. Only then did I dare step back in the tub and turn on the faucets for the shower. I scrubbed until my skin was red, finally obtaining a measure of relief from the burden of uncleanliness.

When I had dried, I went to the bedroom to dress. The slacks were folded on the bed, and I eyed them several times, feeling skittish and excited. I slipped them on, carefully closing the zipper against my skin and smoothing the fabric down my thighs. I pulled the big mirror out of the closet, leaned it against the wall and stepped back.

Something flitted behind me, and I whirled around, too late to catch sight of it. I returned to the image in front of me, unable to take my eyes from the slacks. Their color had darkened from rose to scarlet, and what at first had been attractive now seemed lewd. Again something flickered in the background, and when I turned I thought I glimpsed a serpentine shape, but it disappeared before I could determine its source. The bedroom was growing dimmer, and I switched on a lamp. The slacks seemed now an even deeper red, and I thought I could see tiny hairs on the surface. A moment later these hairs began to beat in time with my heart.

I wondered if this were an effect of the light, which, despite the lamp, seemed inexorably to be failing. At the same time, the room was getting stuffy, and I found that even deep breaths were catching in my throat. In the mirror my face was becoming less and less distinct, its individual features being drained of life by a darkness whose origin I had yet to guess. This darkness grew until all else in the room was on the verge of extinction. I wrenched myself from the mirror, seeking an escape beyond the opacity of the room and its oppressive walls. But all was in shadow, and suddenly I realized the source of the darkness. I had placed the mirror against the north wall, inadvertently making it a window through which the menace from next door could pass. My preoccupation with the pants had made me forget, and I was in grave jeopardy.

I forced a laugh, but it was a cry of panic that echoed in the room. Nocturnal beasts lay in corners, and I began to sense thready digits groping for my flesh. The cloth on my skin was alive, the hairs glowing in the darkness, and in a siege of terror I leapt at the mirror, the gate, striking it with the heel of a shoe I had torn from my foot. There was a hiss, an instant of violence, and then the glass screeched and shattered. Splintered eyes flew through the air, settling to the ground in dangerous patterns. The room seemed momentarily to brighten, but then the darkness became total and I collapsed to the floor.

I forget much of what happened after that, except that by the time Curtis arrived home I had disposed of the glass and the mirror casing. I was wearing a different pair of slacks, and even now am not quite sure what became of the others. I tried to explain what had happened but was hardly coherent: large pieces of the afternoon had somehow vanished from my memory. I felt self-conscious and not a little embarrassed. Curtis was grumpy from a bad day at work, and it was easiest to forget the whole matter. We had a quick dinner and went to bed early. That night the nightmares returned.

Over the course of the next weeks the situation at home deteriorated. Curtis's job became more and more demanding, and many evenings passed when I ate dinner alone. Tanya reacted by clinging more to me, though whether this was due to Curtis's absence or the other pressures that were building, I'm not sure. Regardless, her newfound insecurity came at a time when I had little extra to give. I was engaged in a battle of my own.

Shortly after the episode with the mirror I quit my summer post with the university. It had become too difficult to concentrate on even minor tasks when the safety of my home and family was at stake. I resolved to do what was necessary to eliminate the threat.

As I began to spend more time at home, I realized how timely my decision had been. New intrusions were coming daily from the neighboring house, and it took every effort to neutralize them. After removing all mirrors and reflecting glass, I scrubbed the walls with cleanser. Even so, discolored areas remained, and there were cracks through which cold drafts blew even on windless days. On the floor I found several patches of rug that had been unnaturally frayed and a carpet tack that had somehow worked its way loose. Dust and lint seemed to accumulate ever faster, and I had to begin vacuuming twice daily. That, I think, was in October. Two weeks ago the smell began.

It started in the basement but after a day or two came to occupy the whole house. I presumed at first an impaction of unusually thick waste in one of the sewage lines, but neither toilet nor sink in all the house was affected. Next I imagined that some hitherto unknown septic system, only now discovered, liberated, perhaps, by the deep burrowing of some rodent had been disrupted. The supposition was preposterous, but at the time I was quite willing to go to any length of self-deception. And yet even then I suppose I knew the source.

The stench was constant, though its quality varied by location. In our bedroom it hung like a vast and sulphurous cloud, impossibly foul, such that I could not enter without convulsions taking my stomach. In the living room it hovered acridly along the edges, waiting until I was well inside to gag me. And on the lower level of the house the air was fetid and moist, a rank breeding ground for mildew and other malodorous fungi.

Night and day the odors remained, assaulting me and poisoning the air. By this time I had no doubt as to their source, and the willfulness of the attack I took as a test of my resolve. I doubled, then re-doubled my cleaning efforts. No longer was it sufficient to have the floors clean. The walls too had to be washed, as well as ceilings, closets and windows. I bought scents to freshen each room and several times daily sprayed the air with pungent aerosols. I began to change my clothes more frequently to prevent the odors from staying on the fabrics, and my own body I washed morning, afternoon and evening. My determination had an effect, for I was able at length to eliminate the stench, though success depended on my constant and unyielding vigilance. I deemed such an expense small, and became infused with renewed vigor and hope. At last I was recovering my powers and would soon again be in control.

At these prospects I began to feel better, and for a few days believed even that the problems were solved. In retrospect, I see how hope had replaced reality, but I can hardly be blamed for wanting a respite from the turmoil of those days. Not only was I fighting the battle for our home, but I was drawn increasingly into conflicts with Tanya and Curtis. Neither seemed to share my concerns for our safety. On the contrary, they seemed to withdraw, leaving me more and more isolated, and this at a time when I needed their support more than ever. I tried at first to understand, reasoning that Curtis was under pressure at work and could not be burdened by other problems. And Tanya was just a child. How could she possibly be held responsible for this deterioration?

Nonetheless, my suspicions grew, and in an act of near desperation I decided to confront them, beginning with my daughter.

The next day I kept her home from the sitter, forcing her to stand against the north wall of her bedroom. I did not spray that morning and waited until the stench had become unbearable. Then I asked if she noticed the bad smell.

She shook her head, a false look of innocence on her face.

"Don't lie to me," I said, and grabbed her, pressing her nose to the wall. "Smell it."

Deliberately, she began to cry, and I slapped her. She cried more, but by then I could no longer bear it and rushed from the room. That night Curtis told me I was sick.

I suppose I should have expected it, realizing the distrust in which we now seemed to hold each other, but it struck me as a heartless and untimely jibe. Had he been laboring as I had, struggling moment by moment to maintain a semblence of order in our home, I might have dismissed his judgment as rash but unavoidable. But this was not the case, and clearly his comment was intended to provoke and isolate me further. It had its desired effect, and the verbal fight that ensued turned physical, then violent. Hard blows were struck, and in a sudden flash I recognized the true face of an enemy. Crying, clawing, I drove it from the house.

That was days ago. Now I am here alone. At times I think Tanya is with me, other times not. There is a shape in her crib that moves subtly. Perhaps it is trying to speak. At night it glows faintly . . . indeed, is the single luminosity within the ever-darkening shadow. I bring food, saving what is not eaten for myself. She has become a good child and no longer cries. Perhaps the tongue has been taught by the other worms.

The house next door has come back, and I realize how shallow my understanding has been. Wood and plaster, nails, glass, none of these carries a threat to my person. Nor does the house itself, for in truth it is but an agent. What opposes me is the realm of which it is born, its past, present and future. What lives resides in the earth, in the deformed seeds of plants and weeds, sprouting and sending roots against me, malicious tendrils like earthworms burrowing through the soil to penetrate my walls and sully.

I have covered the windows with linoleum. I attempt to keep my house clean.

Yesterday I devised a way to defeat the odors. With the long-stemmed matches Curtis keeps beside our fireplace I cauterized my nostrils. There was a brief slice of pain, but now I am immune to nasal challenge. My will hardens. Daily I am growing more potent.

This morning I found the red pants. They were lying in the closet beneath dirty linens. Their color seems faded, and along the legs are glistening trails. Spots of mold dot the seams in obvious patterns.

With dawning recognition I slip them on, fastening them at the waist. I extinguish all lights. The fabric clings like a web to my skin as I go to lie in the closet. In a darkness as dense as my will I pull Curtis's remaining clothes from the hangers, settling among them without fear. Thus reposed, a beacon now, a bait, I offer myself in sacrifice.

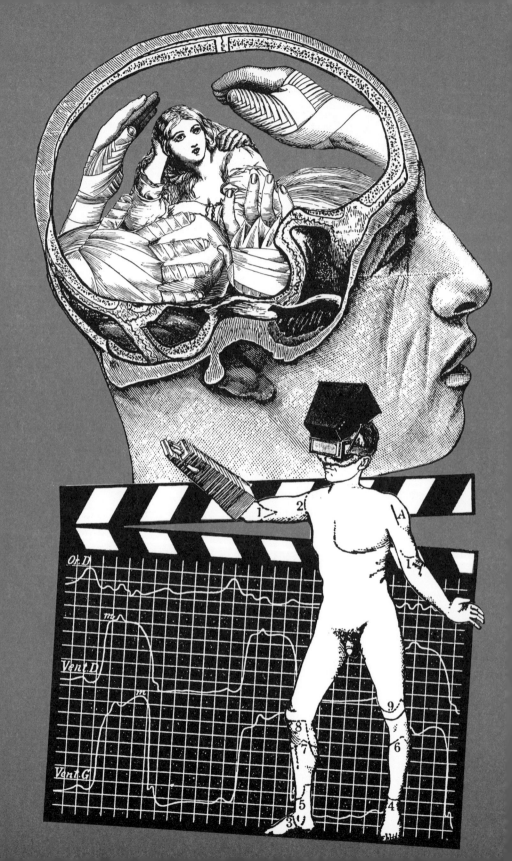

THE GLITTER AND THE GLAMOUR

Face long like a capsule. Mirror eyes.

"Hello, Mr. Crane. Any problems today?"

I blink.

"No? Good. Just stopping by to check." A face looms, and a feeling of confidence surges in me.

"The heart's a jaguar. And the rest . . . I'm sure you'll be pleased." He touches a button and my chest starts to jump. My eyes pop. He nods.

"You see? Younger than springtime. You know you're the oldest one still living?"

Let him go, Sandra. You know he wanted it this way. We'll build a life, a home, right here. On his grave.

"You got started, what?" He pulls a book from his pocket and flips the pages. Animals rustle in the bushes. "More than eighty years ago."

I blink twice and try to smile. A hand flies to my face.

"Please don't do that, Mr. Crane. We've got your lips tied back until the new teeth grow in. Popularity depends on the integrity of the labio-gingival junction. It's better if you just try to relax. Do you understand?"

Two blinks.

"Good. I'll be going now. By the way, I won't be back again

this run. I'm due to be kildaired. Faith in the innocent youth and all that." Deep and mellow, his voice is a drug.

Thank you, doctor, thank you. I blink and blink until my lids are sore. He smiles on me.

"Nature loves excellence. I hope to see you again." He turns and leaves, and I lay back in the comfort of his winning style.

After awhile another man comes in, making noises to himself. He nears me, and a dark moon presses. I flatten. He shakes his head.

"Too bad, man."

He disappears. An arm floats up, fiddles with a bottle. White sleeve, stain of sweat in the armpit. Loretta's pants. On the beach, where I loved her. The sharp brine, that other smell. Plastic now, rubber snakes down my nose. Some jungle here. I sleep.

Later on, Randy comes in. He swallows air and clucks down in his throat when he's nervous. I know it's him before he speaks.

"Hi, Swan." He flashes a smile and gold coins fall from his mouth. "I brought the contract."

I see bright lights. Randy's rainbow face hovers in the air. He waves a white goose.

"They're ready for you in two weeks. Got a hot one this time. Name's Charlene."

Charlene? Ashes. Hairless knee. Marry you, beauty queen? Who's Charlene?

"She's tracked for minor fame. Athletic, domestic, speaking parts limited to kindness, worry and support. They want to show her with you. Give her a start."

Charlene, I love you. Marry me. We'll hire someone to take out the trash. I'll be your father, a milkshake date, the boy next door with freckles. It's always been you, Rhonda. Your legs are my dream. A waltz through champagne, they made my hair pink for you.

Randy's pancake blots out the light. "You're really something, Swan. My grandmother swooned for you, and my mom too. Now

Sara's starting in, and she just turned twelve. You're the standard, all right."

Flashbulb eyes, his voice is syrup. For breakfast it's my silhouette. Look, the bridge of my nose, it's been fixed for you. I've got a gun, Celise. I'm a cowboy, riding hard, giving my chaps, my spurs for love.

"I'll tell them you'll be ready." A leather fish flops on my hand. "Here, I'll help you sign."

Scratch, scratch. A piece of skin sloughs off. Randy clucks and moves back. The light dives to my face.

"Got to be going, champ. You take care. See you in a couple." He leaves, and I settle in with the snakes and the magic.

Sometime later, the dark moon returns. He lifts something through the air and wraps it around my arm. Poonka, poonka, poonka. Black moss clings to his chin. His eyes move from side to side. I blink and pull up my lips.

"That's right, man, laugh it up. Glitter's what you know, glitter's how you go." His face grows. "Them ladies don't want you, robot man. They don't want you now, not no prune man, no dried up stick, even if you fancy and own a fast car and got diamonds in your teeth and glitter in your eyes. Ain't no one ever did, 'cept maybe the other robots, the ones s'posed to love you, the fangs how they kiss, your magazine bowtie, your ass. They kiss your smile, star man, and how does it feel, did they stick rubies in your jewels? I heard they wrapped you in diamonds, did they tie you down? What leash? You tied now, movie man, tied down bad, and ain't no one coming to kiss your hand."

A horizontal gap opens in the moon, and I see rows of milk-white pillars, a diamond cut in each one. Gravity tugs at my chest.

"Sorry for you, man. How long? How long now?"

He sinks to the side, and I breathe. Old bones, a beggar for life. White flags flutter, or are they wings?

*   *   *

"For you, sir. It's the studio." He puts the box on the table next to my bed.

"Thank you, Ackerman. A bit more jelly, please. And gather up the crumbs."

I brush my finger over the switch, and the tube hisses on. A fat face fills the screen.

"Swan. Good to see you. You look well."

"I am, Billy." I pat the corner of my mouth with the napkin, then let it fall to the tray. "Randy tells me you're ready to roll."

"We've got a winner this time, Swan. Name's Charlene, you might know her . . ."

I give him blankness.

"No? I heard they did her in the same place."

"As a rule, Billy, I don't leave the room."

His crooked eyes are eager for more. He always wants more. The silence grows.

"Right. Well, that's what they said. Anyway, just called to check in. You look good. Let's see the profile.'"

I give him the left, lifting my chin a fraction. The nostrils flare. The sea, Stella, it draws me. I taste the salt, the fish in my veins. The sheep are no good, the dirt clots my spirit. I need water, Stella, and you.

"I like it, Swan. The chin's perfect, and I like what they did with the forehead. Bold, yet thoughtful. It's what we've been gearing up to."

"When do we start, Billy?"

"Tomorrow. They've been shooting Charlene already. We put out an augmentation of you and her playing tennis, splashed it up a bit. It should hit the tubes in a day or two."

I smile. "I'm already falling in love with her."

"Good. You might as well be happy."

"I'm always happy, Billy." When I'm around you. I can't help it, Doris. You light me up. I'll eat your hand. Out of it. Candy, candy.

"You amaze me, Swan." He shakes his head. "They broke the mold after they made you. They really did."

This stirs me. "I'm just a regular guy, Billy. Really, just regular."

"Right. Well look, I gotta go. You take care, and I'll see you tomorrow."

The picture goes dead.

I get up and stroll around the room, feeling the body. Young again, lungs flushed, skin taut. Heart of a youth, and the thoughts are tidy, with just the right amount of memory. At the mirror I see that Billy is right: the face is something new, inspiring. I tighten the buttocks in a pose. Nice. I begin to think of Charlene.

She likes sports, Randy says. I don't know sports, but I will. The body wants them, and the mind. I like Charlene. Already I seem to like her a lot.

I move my arm as though swinging a racquet. I smile into the mirror, and the kliegs bathe me in light. I send them my teeth, my lips, my manly scent. The fans make a breeze in my hair, stirring it. Terry, come home with me. I'll feed the pigs and bring home the bacon. I'll give up the spotlight if you'll shine your love light. All this, don't you see, it just doesn't mean a thing without you.

"Excuse me, sir. Is there anything else?"

Ackerman, and his closeted eyes. He holds a silver tray spattered with bread crumbs.

"Draw my bath please."

"Of course. Cherry?"

"Yes."

He goes into the bathroom then returns, a crumpled package of bath beads lying on the plate with the crumbs.

"The bath is running, sir. The foam is rising."

Something about his manner chills me.

"Thank you. You may go."

After a few minutes I go to the bath and turn off the faucets. The air is sweet, I'm coming. Ripe fruit, yes, I take a draught. I croon, then slip into the cherry sea with Esther and her hundred laughing mermaids.

*   *   *

Next day on the set I see Charlene for the first time. She has lively red hair and cozy skin. I imagine a fire dashing up a hill. When we meet, she smiles, hearth and home. Then and there I know that whatever I do, she'll understand.

"Want to go for a walk?" she says, lacing an arm through mine.

"Let's make it a run," I answer, knowing it to be right.

She laughs, and we take off. The sun makes her hair a little too brassy, mine a little too bright, but nevermind, this is love and later on we'll look right.

We talk as we run through the grounds, as people point and stare. Randy's done his job and I smile, letting them see my bold new face, my white teeth. Charlene watches proudly.

"I love to jog," I tell her.

"I understand," she says. "So do I."

"And tennis?"

"Yes, Swan." She smiles. "That too."

I kiss her on the cheek in full stride. "I love you, Charlene. I feel like I've been waiting my whole life for someone like you."

"You make me happy, Swan. Like a high dive or a quiet evening at home."

I smile boyishly and turn into the main street. It is wide and lined with tall palms. In and out we weave, matching each other step for step. I don't care if no one finds us. We'll live on fish, Susan, and coconut milk. I'll build a sandcastle, we'll put up the drawbridge and live there forever.

"I love you."

"I love you, Swan."

"You had brown hair."

"Red, Swan, it's red." She laughs.

"Coconuts."

"Yummy. Let's race to the ocean."

She sprints and I follow, watching out for cars and soldiers and crabs.

Over the next week we work on the movie, the lives merging as I knew they would. To me, public and private are two words for the same thing; I guess I'm lucky that way. One smile does for both, one hairdo, even the shoes can be the same. Work is never a strain because all I have to do is live my life, and living is easy.

The second week of production we get married, and Randy arranges for a really perfect wedding. He has us fly out to Forest Hills, where we have the ceremony on center court. Then Charlene and I lead a group of fans on a jog to the beach. It's summer, and we have an old-fashioned fish fry, Charlene looking great in pink. I wear blue and muscles, and the cameramen aren't lazy. For the finale we water-ski to our yacht, laughing, waving, cameras rolling.

On the deck of the boat is Ackerman, his narrow face watching the sea.

"Welcome aboard, sir."

"Thank you, Ackerman. You know Charlene."

He bows slightly. "Welcome aboard."

"Thank you. I'm pleased to be part of the crew."

He turns to me with the faintest of smiles. "Champagne, sir?"

"Yes. Two glasses."

"The pink?"

Pink for you, Rhonda. To match your eyes. There's no step I wouldn't do for you. I'm just a dancin' fool.

"They're playing a waltz."

"Sir?"

"A waltz. One, two, three, one, two, three." I reach for my partner and we begin to spin around the floor. The music is clear, but she's stiff in my arms. I keep stumbling and stepping on toes.

"Darling," I apologize, "I'm a little tired. Let's stop for a moment. Perhaps a bit of champagne?"

Lines worry her face, then disappear as she kisses me. "Pink, darling?"

A memory winks out.

"Yes, pink."

"Ackerman, two glasses. Chilled, please."

As he shifts his eyes to her, I sense a change. He nods crisply. "Of course."

Charlene turns to me, the pink of her outfit catching the orange of the sun. Bright fish dive in and out of her shimmering body.

"Esther," I murmur, on fire. "I love you."

There's no honeymoon because we want to get the movie out. Maybe that's the mistake. The more we work, the more my wives come to visit. I have less and less time with Charlene. We'll be in the middle of a tennis game, or skiing, or swimming, and Celise will come by, sweet as a lariat round a doggie's neck, or Stella, the good earth etched into the lines on her face, and what can I do? I'm an honest man, and a good husband. I don't cheat, I don't play around. Why should I? To me, love is a pure and simple thing. What I say on screen is how I am in life. It is my life.

Charlene understands this. She understands me, doesn't begrudge a few moments on the prairie, on the old double-masted schooner, in the dancehall with the band. She smiles and waits for me to come back, then slams a serve or makes a pretty volley my way. She's as good as gold, as precious as the others.

Randy tells me to relax, but Billy's mad. He says I'm not paying attention, the studio's losing money.

"Charlene!" he's been yelling at me. "Charlene, Charlene, Charlene! Not Terry, Swan. Or Doris, or Stella, or any of them. They're not here, none of them. This is Charlene. Charlene!"

I know that. How could I not? Of course this is Charlene bronze smile skin. My love, forty match game. My wife.

But what am I supposed to do, Billy, when Esther laughs me into the water, when Rhonda shimmies her silk hips? I'm a gentleman, and these are my wives too. If I have to rope, I will, or eat fish if it's salt. I can be blind, or a farmer. I'll build castles and coconuts and live there, candy and hands clapping at night. If it

takes that, I'll do it. I'll do more, yes, I will. I'll sing and ride and
swim, diamonds in my teeth, flocks of swans, and glitter. I can
dance, and my smile is gold. My arms are wings, and I can fly.

THE PROMISE OF WARMTH

The belly skin is cool, and warming. It lays on bark. Hunger, warming. A lid lifts. An eye watches. It waits.

A low roar grinds in the distance. In the clearing it is bright and soundless. No cry of bird, no leap of rodent. Heat, mid-day, wilting. Silence.

A butterfly shivers by, vanishes behind a broad leaf. Another appears from shadow, flashing blue wing eyes. A beautiful creature, its movements are coarse, the spasms of the insect mind. It flutters through a veil of vines, lighting on a crimson flower. Once, twice it bats its wings, then jerks into the air. It nears the waiting branch.

A ray of sun darts past leaf and limb, touching the butterfly, pinning it. The beat of a wing. An eye moves, a mouth, a flicker of flesh. The tongue snaps, strikes, retreats. The butterfly is gone. The eye closes, the hunger soothed. The body is content, and warming.

"I'm nervous," said Roger. Jill fumbled with her wallet, trying to make the oversized paper bills fit in the slot made for the long and narrow U.S. dollars.

"I really am."

She looked up to see if he was serious. He was, in his fashion, or so she decided. She stuffed the unfinished business in her back pocket.

"C'mon, it'll be fine." She laid a hand on his arm, but the heavy lines remained above his eyes. She changed her tactic.

"No, you're right, it's going to be horrible. We'll probably sit on the beach all day, and if it doesn't rain, it'll be too hot, or if it's not too hot the mosquitoes'll eat us alive, or if there're no mosquitoes, there'll be something else in the sand, chiggers or no-see-ums, or something worse, tropical, invisible, a venom that doesn't make you die, just makes you itch, and swell, and itch some more . . ." She took a breath, ready to go on.

Being the comedian was not natural to her, it was not the flavor of her other relationships. She learned how to tease to make Roger laugh. Laughing, he would sometimes relax the grip he had on himself.

"You're right," he grumbled. "It's going to be just like that." The lines deepened, then suddenly his face lifted. He laughed and grabbed Jill.

"I'm crazy," he said, hugging her. "I know it."

"You are."

"I can't help it. I'm worried that we're not going to have a good time."

"Relax." She took his hand as they walked. "Have a few margaritas."

"You like it when I'm drunk, don't you?"

"I like it when you let go a little."

"I bet you do." He kissed her on the cheek, then moved his lips slowly to her ear, tonguing the entrance.

"Not here, Roger. Let's go back to the hotel."

"C'mon, let's sneak behind one of the bushes. A quickie. Au naturel."

"Someone might see us."

"Let 'em, we got nothing to hide." He reached for her arm, but she held him away.

"Stop playing."

"Relax," he said, twisting the word. "You're so uptight."

She stiffened. With a hurt and angry look she turned away.

Roger watched her leave. The sounds of the village, of chickens and children and jukebox music hung in the air. He cursed himself.

"Jill!" he called. "Jill!"

He ran after her, stirring up whirls of dust in the road. He avoided a rock, stubbed his toe on another. When he caught up with her he limped to the side, uttering apologies. She studiously ignored him. Finally he ran ahead and turned back to face her. She had no choice but to stop.

"I'm sorry," he said. "I am. Really."

"Why do you do that?"

"I don't know. I don't mean to hurt you."

"No?"

"I don't. I don't like to."

"Really?" She seemed surprised.

"Really."

"Then stop it. Be nice."

"I'm trying. It's slow, but I'm trying to change."

"Do it soon, okay?"

She touched his arm, then hugged him.

Roger held on with relief.

"Let's go back to the hotel," Jill murmured.

"Yeah. Let's."

"Kiss me first." Her eyes were already closed.

They kissed. Hand in hand they walked back.

The hammock hung between two branches that had twined behind the low wooden sill that served as the hotel's front desk. A man with sleepy eyes lay sunken in it, a leg draped carelessly over the edge. Behind him on the wall were nailed two boards. The top one was painted white and carried the name of the hotel scrawled in bold, irregular letters. LAS TRES CABEZAS. The other was unpainted and weathered. Written across in Spanish and English were the words *Checkout time 2 P.M. Do not be late.* To the side of the desk was a large cooler filled with Mexican beer and a variety of soft drinks. A child, a young girl, stood in the corner sipping a Coke. Her dark eyes followed Roger as he came to the counter. He put the room key down then leaned forward, smiling at the man in the hammock.

"Buenos días."

"Días." A grunt came from the vicinity of the man's mouth.

"Cómo está?"

"Aquí, no mas."

Roger nodded and smiled, while he thought what to say next. He had talked to the man, Carlos, the afternoon before. They had chatted about the village, its peacefulness, the foreigners who came to visit. The conversation had been lively and Carlos, animated. Now, even though it was morning and the heat had not yet risen with its heavy hand, the man seemed tired.

"Hot, huh?" Roger said, lifting his straw hat and brushing his hair, already wet.

"Makes hotter later," the man said with an effort.

"Hard night?" Roger asked, strangely curious why the man was so sluggish this early.

Carlos moved his head a fraction, not enough to disturb his torpid peace, and slit his eyes in Roger's direction. His mouth dropped open and the tongue came out to circle his dry lips. A low, echoing sound rose from his throat, and it took Roger a moment to understand that he was speaking.

"I am tired, hijo. Still sleeping. Come back later. Hotter. For some, heat makes . . ." He sighed. ". . . come alive." He fell back into his daze.

Roger stared. He caught a glimpse of the girl. She was watching him.

"Is he okay?" he asked. "Está bien?"

She sipped the Coke.

"El," he pointed. "Bien? Está bien?"

She sipped. Finally, she nodded.

Roger frowned and turned away. He was shaking his head when Jill came down the stairs to his right. She had a bag over her shoulder and was dressed for the beach.

"What's wrong?"

"The old man," he motioned. "Carlos. He looks sick."

"Did you talk to him?"

"Yeah. He says he's just tired. That he wakes up later, when it's hotter."

"Weird. The heat puts me to sleep."

"Me too."

They started to walk.

"You worried about him?"

"Not really. I'd just like to understand."

"Yeah. Well, give it time. Maybe we'll feel that way too after we've been here awhile."

"Maybe," he said, unconvinced.

"Don't worry about it." She threaded an arm behind his back. "We're here for us, Roger, not him."

"Yeah, I guess you're right."

They walked for awhile in silence.

"You want to stop in the market?" said Roger. "Pick up something for later."

"Sounds good."

They steered toward the center of town, past a waterless fountain, turning right at the cobbled road that led to the market. They passed a burro strapped down beneath a pile of wood, and a bit further they came alongside a woman carrying a pig. The pig squealed, and the woman let it drop to the ground, holding it close to her side with a short rope wrapped around its neck. Jill stooped down, making clicking sounds with her tongue to attract the pig's attention. The woman gave her an odd look and tugged it away. Jill stood up, feeling foolish.

They passed an outdoor barber shop, a simple wooden chair sitting on the dusty ground with a jagged mirror hanging from a tree next to it. Further along was a long white building with *Funerales* written in big black letters and several open wooden coffins lying in the shed at one end. A man was selling peanuts on the stoop in front, measuring them out with an old Campbell's soup can. The market was just across the street.

They entered and wound their way past cluttered stalls until they came to the open space in the center. It was full of women, many standing at tables piled high with vegetables and fruits. Others sat cross-legged on the ground, food spread before them on an old cloth, a piece of muslin. The place was crowded and noisy. Jill and Roger bumped their way from stand to stand, touching and smelling until Roger had satisfied himself that they had found the best papaya in the marketplace. He paid for it and they turned to leave, when something caught the corner of his eye.

Nearby, a dark, wiry man was squatting on the ground. He wore a tattered shirt and bruised hat, which was tilted forward on his head. At his feet lay a coarse gunny sack. He had raised the lip with one hand and was searching inside with the other. The woman who stood over him bent down, following his movements with her eyes. The man said a quick word and she nodded. He pulled back his hand. In it, grasped tightly, were two lizards. Big ones. Their claws had been tied back, and their swollen white bellies moved in and out like tiny bellows. They were alive.

Roger watched, transfixed, as the man lifted the creatures by the tails, swinging them toward the woman. She extended a hand, and with the tips of her fingers stroked the lacy green backs, the heads. Gently, she squeezed the bellies. Roger shivered, and the woman looked up. Her wizened face strained against the glare of the morning. Suddenly she smiled. The few teeth still in her mouth were outlined in gold.

She said something that he couldn't quite hear, but he mumbled some words as if he understood. She smiled again, then turned back to the man and spoke rapidly. Once or twice she gestured in Roger's direction. When she finished, the man nodded. He gave her the animals and stood up. He was not tall. With a hand he beckoned to Roger.

His eyes were black, the lids lashless and hardly visible. When he grinned, his face cracked like a desert.

"Qué necesita, señor?"

"Nada," Roger mumbled.

The man smiled. "Nada?"

Roger shook his head. He felt queasy.

The man placed a hand on his shoulder and knelt down, pulling Roger with him. Jill stood nearby, uninvolved and bored.

The man grasped the edge of the sack with one hand and thrust the other deep inside. Slowly he drew it out.

Roger's heart quickened. A bead of sweat grew at his lip. In the man's hand a thick tail appeared. Bound legs, then a back, humped and green. Unconsciously, Roger reached for it. He touched the cool and puckered skin, stroking the ridge of the spine. He fingered the forehead, the blunt snout, and lifted the chin, turning it until the creature's head faced his own.

The eyes blinked and remained open. The tongue danced out, brushed his hand, disappeared. Roger stared. The sun beat on his neck. Dimly, he felt its warmth.

A hand touched his back. It startled him.

"Huh?"

"I said I'm getting tired of standing here. If you want to stay, I'll meet you at the beach."

He shook his head, trying to clear it. "No, wait. I'm ready. I'll come." He stood up, and felt faint. He put a hand on Jill's shoulder.

"You okay?"

"A little dizzy . . ."

He waited for it to pass.

"I'm all right now."

"You sure?"

"Yeah. I'm okay."

"Good. Let's go then."

She started out, and in a moment Roger followed. After a few steps he stopped, briefly, and looked back. A woman behind him was weighing a bunch of bananas, and next to her another was dusting flies from pieces of cut pineapple. Beyond were more people, and in the midst of the crowd he caught a glimpse of the old man and woman squatted down over the gunny sack. Turning away, he hurried to catch up with Jill.

*   *   *

Even in the shade the heat dominated. It hung on the air like balls of cotton. Jill wiped her forehead and put down her book. She reached for the beer. It was lukewarm, cool by comparison to her mouth. She squeezed a lime onto the metal top, sucked the juice off the rim, chased it with a gulp from the can. She wiped off the foam from her lip and took another drink. She was content.

Next to her Roger's body was sprawled face down in the sand. "You're getting burnt," she said.

"Mmm."

"The backs of your legs are really red." Unconsciously, she moved her chair into the center of the jalapa's shifting shadow.

"You should come in out of the sun. Or put on some cream."

"Too much trouble," he grunted.

"Really. You should."

"Uh-huh."

"Stubborn."

"What?"

"Nothing."

He stirred, raising his head. "You called me stubborn."

"You are."

"I'm relaxing."

"Good."

"I am." He flopped back down on the sand.

"What'cha thinking?" Jill asked.

"Nothing."

"A peso."

He smiled. "Lizards."

"What about lizards?"

"They know how to relax. When it's hot, they just lie in the sun. Eat when they feel like it. When it's cold, they don't do anything."

"Sounds nice."

"Yeah."

"Unless you get eaten by a bird."

"They wouldn't eat a big one. Not a big one."

"Like an iguana."

"Yeah. They wouldn't eat an iguana. Too big."

Jill drank more of her beer. "What made you think of them?"

"I don't know. It seems like a pretty good life. Eat, sleep, sunbathe . . ."

She laughed. "Sounds like the vacation's doing some good."

"And another thing," he said, leaning toward her. "They've got fast tongues."

He flashed his out and licked her calf. "Yuck!" He spat on the ground. "You taste terrible!"

"Sea and Ski Number Six," she laughed. "Next time try the lips."

He tried to drown the taste with some beer, then jumped up and raced to the water. Splashing in like a child, he swam off. Jill watched, shaking her head. It was mid-day, sweltering. Roger was the only one in the water.

She caught sight of a man plodding up the beach. He had a narrow white towel draped over an arm and was carrying a tray with drinks. She lifted her beer, pointing to it.

"Una mas," she said.

He nodded, and Jill finished off the can. Then she lay back and closed her eyes, letting the heat and alcohol take her away.

Later, when it was time to leave, after gathering the towels and throwing away the remains of the papaya, she went looking for Roger. He had come back, talked a little, then bounded off again.

She called his name. And again, impatiently. She had nearly decided to go back alone when she saw some tracks in the sand. They made a wide rut, as if some broad object had been dragged along the beach. It began where she had last seen Roger lying in the sun. Jill threw the day bag over her shoulder and followed the trail.

For a short distance it ran parallel to the shore, passing over a hump of sand before making a sharp turn toward the water. It gave out at the base of a low rock, the first of several stretching in a line into the bay. The ones close to shore were covered by urchins and tiny mollusks. The tide at that hour, near sunset, was low, and the rocks were dry. She climbed up.

The surface was not steep, but it was sharp and in shadow. She picked her way carefully, in a few minutes reaching the top. The low sun lit her face, for a moment blinding her. When her eyes cleared, she looked down to the other side.

It was flatter, the far edge sliding into the surf. Some cormorants mingled with pelicans, oiling their wings. Off to one side lay Roger, sprawled belly down on the rock. His head faced the dying sun.

"Roger? Roger, are you all right?"

She began to climb down, putting the cutting pieces of rock out of her mind. The big birds leapt from their roosts, screeching.

"Roger!"

She reached him, touched his back.

"Roger?" She lifted his head. "Roger! Answer me!"

He blinked, then slowly stretched. Straightening his arms, he pushed himself up.

His chest and belly were covered with scratches, streaks of dried blood. He turned his head from side to side.

"Jill," he said dreamily.

She waited, holding her breath.

"It was so peaceful. The rocks were so warm."

Her throat felt tight. "Are you all right?"

He blinked. "Is something wrong?"

"Stop joking, Roger."

"No, really. What's wrong?" He looked at her, saw the fury rising. "Jill . . ."

"Stop it," she screamed. "Stop it! Stop!" She began to cry.

"I don't understand," he said helplessly. "What did I do?"

"You tell me."

"I don't know." He strained, trying to think. "Because I went off by myself?"

She was trembling.

"I didn't mean to be gone so long, Jill. It just happened. I guess I fell asleep. The sun felt so good . . ."

"I thought you were dead."

"I should have said something. Should have told you where I was going."

"What did you do, crawl the whole way?"

He fingered some of the cuts, then grinned sheepishly. "I guess I did, didn't I? Nutty, huh?"

"Something's wrong, Roger. You scare me."

"I don't mean to."

She looked at him accusingly.

"I'm sorry," he said. "Really."

"Let's go back, okay?" She wiped her eyes, then helped him up. "You should get cleaned up."

"They don't hurt."

"Don't start again, Roger."

"Really . . ."

She gave him a look and he shut up. She turned and began climbing, slowly, carefully. Roger waited until she was over the top then scurried after her.

By the time they had showered and dressed, it was well past sunset. The pink had become violet, and bright stars were beginning to poke through the sky. Tired fishermen brought late boats to their berths. In the bay's reaches, where the ebb had already erased the shallow fingers of water, skiffs sat in the mud, moored to a piling or the branch of a tree. Women and children bargained for the day's catch, for vela, calamare, huachenango. A young boy played with a sailfish, opening and closing the sail like a fan. On the porch outside their room Jill stood with a beer. She took a sip and leaned against the rail. She stared out.

Roger appeared, shirtless and barefoot, and walked forward, slipping his arms around her. He kissed her on the neck. She murmured and turned to him. They touched lips, briefly, then Roger pulled away. He yawned.

"I'm sleepy."

"You got too much sun. How's your chest?"

He touched it. "Feels fine."

"Did you put on some cream?"

He nodded, but to Jill's eye he needed more. His skin looked wrinkled and loose, as though the upper layers were sliding off the ones beneath.

"You're so dry," she said, and ran a finger over his ribs. The skin puckered, and a piece slid off. She jerked her hand away and stared, as it floated to the ground.

"I am, aren't I?" He rubbed an arm, making a shower of scales.

Tentatively, she touched the place where the skin had come off. "Does it hurt?"

"Uh-uh. Not at all."

She frowned. "Something's the matter, Roger. I think you should see a doctor."

"I feel all right."

"You're getting too much sun. You're acting weird."

"I like the sun."

"You're not used to it."

"It doesn't bother me." He stifled a yawn.

"Fine," she said. "Do it your way." She took a drink and stared at the water.

"C'mon, Jill, don't be like that."

She started to reply then stopped herself. She sighed. "I'm worried about you, Roger. That thing today at the beach frightened me."

"It's okay." He hugged her. "Promise."

"Really?"

"Really. I'm just a little tired."

"Maybe you'll feel better after we eat. Why don't you get dressed so we can go?"

In the room he put on a shirt and sandals, and they walked the short distance to the restaurant. For dinner they ordered fresh fish, rice and tortillas. Jill ate with a vengeance, while Roger hardly touched his plate. He felt more like sleeping than eating and by the end of the meal stopped fighting the urge. His head drooped to the side and he closed his eyes.

Jill finished quickly, paid the bill, then shook him awake. It wasn't easy, but eventually she pulled him to his feet. Half-carrying, half-dragging him, she finally got him to the hotel.

It was early, and the children were still up. A boy at the desk handed her the key to the room. He smiled and twirled his finger in the air. Jill smiled back, assuming that it meant *drunk* or something like it, and shouldered Roger toward the stairs. Out of the corner of her eye she saw the old man draped heavily in the hammock. Next to him was the girl with the dark eyes. She was staring.

Jill bit her lip and turned away. Sucking in her breath, she heaved Roger toward the room.

Jill woke the next morning to the sound of roosters. Slits of light played through the wooden shutters that were flattened against the screens. They cut down some of the heat, less of the noise, but they were better than nothing.

She kicked off the single sheet and groped to the toilet. When she was done, she crossed to the window and pushed down the lever. Light rushed in, too much of it, and she slammed the shutter closed.

She rubbed her eyes and began to gather clothing. Next to her, Roger slept.

She dressed and quietly left the room. It was mid-morning, and the fishing boats had already gone. The tide was coming in. Jill yawned and stretched. It was time for breakfast.

She found a restaurant close by and ordered eggs, bacon, toast and coffee. She ate slowly, thinking about Roger. She resolved that if he wasn't any better she'd get him to a doctor. It lifted her spirits. She paid the bill and returned to the room.

When she opened the door, she saw that Roger was up. He was leaning against a wall, his back to her. His arms were outstretched, his hands flattened on the smooth surface. A grating sound, fingernails on stucco, splintered the air.

"What are you doing?"

His arms jerked in and out.

"Roger?"

"Wha?"

"What's going on?"

"Nothing."

"I can't hear you."

"Nothing's going on." His voice was coarse.

"Will you turn around, I can barely hear you."

His head tilted to the side. "Just a second."

She waited uneasily, watching. His jaw moved in and out, and his palms rubbed the wall. Slowly, he turned, lowering his arms with an effort. The tip of his tongue darted out, licked his lip, flew back into his mouth. He smiled timidly.

"Morning."

"It's almost noon."

"No wonder I'm so hungry."

"What were you doing, Roger?"

"What do you mean?"

"I mean, why were you lying against the wall?"

"I don't know. Just playing around I guess. Seeing what it was like."

"What *what* was like?"

"I don't know." He shrugged. "It doesn't matter. No big deal."

"I don't like this, Roger. Something's wrong. I'm taking you to a doctor."

"It's just vacation, Jill."

"You're acting too weird." She stepped toward him and reached out. With a start she drew her hand back. When she touched him again, her fingertips were trembling.

"What's the matter?"

"Your skin . . ."

"What? What, Jill?"

"It's cold."

"Make it warm." He came closer. "Please."

His nostrils flared, sending dry puffs of air to her cheeks. His tongue flicked out, touched her hair, her ear. She shivered and came against him. Clumsily, he began to undress her. His fingers were awkward, and she had to help. She pulled off her shirt, then kicked down her shorts.

They stood naked, facing each other. Roger made a sound deep in his throat. His breathing was fast. Jill lifted her arms and held them out. She drew him close. Mindless of the tiny claws on her back and the skin that chafed, she pulled him to the bed.

She came once, riding the tongue that tickled between her legs. It was a strange sensation, a pleasant one, like drifting over warm fields of wheat. The flush left her face but she carried the pleasure for some time after. Roger lay beside her, watching the small movements of her chest. The urgency had left him, and his face held a look of great calm. His eyes were placid; his mind, patient. He murmured to her, hoarsely, from his throat.

"I love you, Jill." She stirred, as if cooled by a breeze.

"Thank you for bringing me here . . ." Gently he lifted his arms.

"For helping me find peace . . ." Feather tongue soft, he touched her a last time.

". . . rest."

He slid from her, off the bed to the floor. Two quick pulls, a swipe at the latch, and he was out the door. He crouched on the steps, head cocked. Suddenly, he jolted up the stairs, his powerful limbs thrusting him forward. He caught the edge of the roof and pulled himself up, then scurried to the center. Mid-day sun soaked him in heat, the promise of warmth forever.

A dragonfly flitted close to his face. His eyes jumped.

Hungry, he thought. Food.

The tongue whipped out, touched a wing, curled back. The buzzing stopped, the eyes stilled, the creature sat, eating.

THE WET SUIT

When Cam first heard the story of his father and the wet suit, he wanted to deny it. He wanted to accuse his mother, who told him, of lying, but that would have been ridiculous. Family lies were wordless ones; they would not be fashioned out of something you could touch and hold in your hand. When Fran said, "I always wondered where he hid this box," and then later, "they're your father's . . . he used these things," Cam knew she wasn't making it up.

It was a bad moment for him, and his mother, kneeling on the other side of the cardboard box, was sympathetic. She too had been victimized by her husband's eccentricity, his brutal singularity. Many times. She was surprised her son didn't know.

They were in the garage, the big two car garage beneath the big five bedroom house. It was a pretty fall morning, crystalline and full of color. The rusty leaves on the maples in back seemed so rich and heavy they would thump when they fell. The poplars in front had already browned out, and their leaves lay scattered on the lawn and driveway, mixing with leaves from other yards. A small pile had built up against the rear wheel of the Mercedes that was parked outside the garage. It was four months since Cam's father had died.

Cam had come up for the weekend to help his mother get the house ready for winter. To replace some worn-out shingles on the roof, put up storm windows, caulk and paint bare spots in the siding. Jobs his father used to do. Fran had asked for his help and he had come. She had told him that there were many tools in his father's workshop that she would never use. He should take them. There was his father's boat, the sixteen-foot fiberglass outboard that sat unused in one half of the big garage. He should take that too. He should take it all. After all, he was the son.

Cam would have come without the enticement. His mother was alone in a big house, a big life without anyone to tell her any-more which doors to open and for how long. He knew the kind of failure she feared. But he wished it could have been simpler, he wished she could have just asked, will you help? Without offering the tools or the boat, without bringing in the lie of possession. He wished she could have asked and he could have answered, simply, yes. But the risk was too great, for both of them. So they stuck to their scheme.

By the time they got to the garage it was Sunday afternoon. Cam had been doing chores all day, and his father's boat was the last. He walked around the frame of the trailer, loosening the brakes on the wheels. His mother watched from the other side of the garage.

"Be careful when you pull it out," she said. "It's wider than you think."

"I'll be careful."

"I can move the Mercedes."

"It's all right."

Cam finished releasing the brakes, then went around to the front where the long arms of the frame under the boat's bow ended in a metal socket. It would have been easy to back his car around and fit the socket over the ball that jutted over his rear fender, then pull the boat out with the car. That was how he and his father had always done it with the Mercedes. But this time he wanted to pull the boat himself, with his own arms and legs.

He joined his hands behind his back and grabbed the socket of the frame, then planted his feet and strained forward. The frame creaked but did not move. He strained harder. Fran folded her arms and watched.

"Why not use the car?" she said, not expecting him to listen.

He didn't. Tightening his shoulder and thigh muscles, he leaned forward until he was nearly parallel to the ground. His face was flushed. He had the brief thought that his father would have been disappointed to see him do such a silly thing. With a groan the wheels began to turn. Once they started it was easy, and in a minute he had the boat in the driveway alongside the Mercedes. He pulled it a little farther up then dropped the socket to the ground. The back of his shirt was streaked with sweat and his forehead was wet.

Fran chose not to make an issue of how close the boat had come to scratching the Mercedes. She was relieved it was out. She stared at the empty space for a minute, thinking of her husband.

"Here," she said absentmindedly, picking up one of several boxes. "This goes with the boat."

Cam came over and took it. Inside were a bunch of wet suits, old and patched with black glue. He walked outside, stepped on the boat frame and tossed the box under the bow.

"You might as well take those too." Fran pointed to a row of waterskis leaning against the back of the garage. "And this." She pushed over another box, full of life preservers and lengths of nylon rope. She stood up, brushing her knees, and looked around. The garage seemed empty, as though something living were gone. She got a little teary-eyed.

Cam came in and the two of them stood quietly together. Afternoon light filtered through the window in the door at the rear of the garage. Outside it dappled the trunk of the maple on the side of the hill. A breeze shook the tree's leaves, making spots of light dance on the garage floor.

Cam stuck his hands in his pockets and shifted his feet. His reticence reminded Fran of her husband, but in Jack the quality had been misanthropic. In Cam it seemed more innocent. She smiled at him.

"The boat will make it harder to drive," she said. "Please be

careful." Urging caution was an oblique expression of her
affection.

Cam looked at her. "What?"

"I said please be careful when you drive home tonight."

He nodded, feeling inexplicably sad. His eyes wandered.
"What's that?" he said, pointing toward the ceiling. Out of reach
above their heads was a box balanced on two of the metal girders
that held up the garage door.

"I don't know," she said curiously. "Get the ladder and we'll
have a look."

While Cam was gone, Fran thought about the box. It was un-
like Jack to put something out of reach, when there was plenty of
space on the floor and walls. He had prided himself on efficiency,
on economy of movement and thrift of thought. He had demanded the same from his family, and with bitterness Fran
remembered how he had intimidated them all. She remembered
his thick-skinned arrogance, his natural feeling of superiority.
Worse, she recalled how she had accepted it, how she had been
content to linger in his shadow. That memory, as she gazed at the
box so irrationally placed, made an anger rise in her. Rise, and be
instantly squelched. It was a shameful thing to carry such feelings
past the grave.

Cam came with the ladder, locked the braces down with his
palm and climbed up. He lifted the box easily, carrying it down
under an arm. When Fran saw how light it was, she had a sudden
thought. She took the box quickly from her son and put it on the
floor. Relishing the moment, she bent back the cardboard flaps.

On the top of the box was another of Jack's wet suits. It was
neatly folded, like a man's shirt, with the zipper facing up. Fran
lifted it out by the shoulders and shook it a little, until the spongy
material hung straight. The first thing she noticed was that the
suit was a woman's: it was darted in front to make room for
breasts. And it had been altered. The crotch strap, which normally hung from the back and snapped in front, was missing.
And there was a skirt on the bottom. Pleated, carefully stitched,
a short pink crinoline skirt.

Fran looked the suit over critically, as a seamstress might examine her work. "I always wondered where he hid this."

Cam frowned. "What is it?"

Fran lay the suit over the edge of the box and fingered the skirt. It was meticulously sewn, with black thread that hid itself in the dark fabric of the suit. He had even used a hemming stitch, and the thought of him poring over it with needle and thread made her want to laugh. She bent over to see what else was in the box, then thought better of it and sat back on her heels. She began to fold the suit.

"What is this stuff?" Cam asked again.

"It's your father's," she answered without looking up. She started to close the cardboard flaps, feeling a kind of loyalty to Jack, a responsibility to protect him that she had never felt while he was alive. Secretly, though, she wanted Cam to stop her. He stopped her.

"What do you mean it's Dad's?" There was an edge to his voice.

"Just that. It's his."

"I want to see."

He reached for the box, but Fran draped her arms over the top, blocking him.

"No," she said firmly. "Let the man rest in peace."

"I want to see it," he repeated. He knelt down and put his hands on the box. For a moment they locked eyes, and then Fran gave in.

Cam took the wet suit out, looked it over himself before letting it fall to the ground. He reached in and pulled out something that resembled an infant's swing. It was a sling of rubber: two wide strips fastened in the middle where they crossed, then tapering over several feet to four narrow ends. Cam held the thing by the ends and stood up. It dangled just above the ground.

"What's this?"

"Put it away, Cam."

"What is it?" he demanded.

"A harness. Your father used it sometimes."

He stared at it a minute, then dropped it on the floor next to the suit. He took out a handful of rubber straps, some short, some long, and then a pair of wet suit boots. He picked up the box and turned it over. Nothing more came out.

Fran sat on her heels, enjoying herself. She found Jack's obsessive ingenuity quite funny, and felt an unexpected wash of affection for him. Cam, on the contrary, was scowling.

"I'm sorry," Fran said, trying to keep a straight face. "I thought everyone knew."

Cam shook his head dumbly.

"Maybe we should talk about it later."

"No. Tell me now."

She composed herself, trying to match her son's gravity. "These . . . things. They're your father's. He used them out back." She paused. "Your brother and sister know. I'm surprised they never told you."

"They didn't. What did he do?"

"Things. Private things. I never looked. I knew about it, but I never wanted to see." The lie was automatic.

"What things?"

She hesitated, then shrugged. "Dierdre told me first. She came to me because she was scared. She was only six or seven. She said that Daddy was out in the back hitting himself. She said he was dressed in a funny-looking wet suit, hitting himself with some straps. He had stuffed something, the boots I guess, into the front of the suit . . ." In her mind she saw it, comical, disturbing.

"He was sitting in that rubber contraption. That harness. He had tied the tops around the low branch of the maple in back, the one on the side of the hill, and he was sitting in that thing like he was being swaddled. And bouncing. Up and down, never quite touching the ground. And groaning."

"C'mon. Dierdre made it up."

"Digger saw it too."

"I don't believe it," Cam said angrily.

"It wasn't easy being your father," Fran said. "He had high standards for himself. For everyone. Someone like that, the pressure always comes out. Some people get violent. At least he kept it to himself."

"But why would he whip himself?"

"I didn't say that," Fran replied pointedly.

"You did."

"Cam." She had not foreseen that he would be so upset. For years she had lived with this thing, had covered it up and turned it into something manageable. A quirk of her husband's. An idiosyncrasy. Another small disappointment in the romance of marriage.

After awhile she began replacing the things in the box. She dropped them in carelessly, as though they were rags. Cam felt there was something improper in the way she did it, but he didn't stop her. He was happy for the moment to have them out of sight.

She closed the flaps and stood up, smoothing the wrinkles out of her skirt. Out the window in the door at the back the sun had sunk lower. The tree on the side of the hill, the maple with the big horizontal branch, was nearly in darkness. Fran hugged herself.

"It's getting late. You should be going."

"What are you going to do with this stuff?"

"I don't know. I'll have to decide."

Cam stuck his hands in his pockets and looked at his feet. "I'd like to take it home," he mumbled. "With the boat."

"I don't think so, honey."

"I'll bring it back."

"No," she said gently. "It should stay here. I'll probably get rid of it."

Cam did not argue. He didn't feel like standing up to his mother. He wanted to be alone.

On the way out, after he had hitched the boat to the car, he went over to say goodbye. She was standing beside the Mercedes, arms folded, teary-eyed but smiling. Cam kissed her on the cheek and they hugged briefly.

"You should get someone to rake up the leaves," he told her. "They can clog the sewer."

"Drive carefully," she said. "If you get tired, stop."

He got in his car, turned on the lights and pulled out. He did not look back. It was dark when he hit the interstate, and he drove home without stopping.

The next day he told his wife, Anita. It was night, and the kids were asleep. She interrupted his story often with questions. She wanted to know details: how long was the skirt? exactly what color? how many straps, and how often did his father do it? What about Fran, what part did she play? Cam finally cut her off.

"I've told you what I know," he snapped. "Please stop asking me questions."

"It's amazing," she said, untangling her hair with one of the kids' brushes. "Old Jack. Upstanding, self-righteous, kinky Jack."

"It's too weird," said Cam. "Sometimes I wonder what planet my family came from."

"Are you ashamed?"

"I don't know what I am. I feel sorry for him. That he had to go and do something like that."

"Maybe he liked it."

Cam frowned. "That's hard to believe. I wonder what he was thinking."

Anita caught something in his voice and took his hand. "Everyone's got something, Cam. It's human nature."

"Is that what it is?" he said harshly. "Tying yourself to a tree and whipping yourself. You call that human nature?"

A few weeks later he called Dierdre on the phone. She was the oldest of the three, four years older than Cam. He asked her about the wet suit.

"Sure I knew. Everyone in the family did."

"I didn't."

"Sure you did. You and I saw him once. You probably just forgot."

"No," he said. "I never saw him. Digger did, and you."

"You were only three or four," Dierdre went on. "You probably don't remember."

"I wouldn't forget something like that, Dee."

"I'm not surprised. It scared the shit out of me."

Cam tried to picture it, but there was nothing. Nothing real. It worried him that he couldn't remember.

"Mom told me what he did out there," he said. "I asked why, and she gave me some bullshit about pressure."

"Did she tell you about the bathing suits?"

"What bathing suits?"

"Every year, sometimes two and three times a year Dad used to buy her bathing suits. This was after she had had the three of us, after she had put on weight and lost her figure. He used to bring home these sexy spandex suits, low cut, strapless, tight all over. The kind you see in magazines. He made special trips downtown to get them. He'd give them to her, I guess sometimes he'd wrap them up, but just as often he'd just hand them to her.

"In the beginning she tried them on, but after one or two times she stopped. She told them they were too tight, which they were. But really she stopped because she felt foolish, but she didn't tell him that."

Dierdre paused, and Cam kept the receiver tight against his ear. In a moment she continued.

"She told me though. Constantly. She felt embarrassed and humiliated. Each time he brought one to her she threw it out. According to Mom, he didn't even notice. He kept buying the suits and bringing them home. I guess he thought that eventually she'd give in, but the more he did it the more resistant she got. Their sex life took a dive around then. I think that's when Dad started his little number in the backyard."

"She didn't say anything about the suits," Cam said.

"I'm not surprised. I doubt it's something she likes remembering."

"But I asked her why," he persisted, hurt by his mother's lack of trust. "She could have said something."

"She's embarrassed. Maybe she doesn't make the connection. You know how Mom is."

"But why the whip, Dee? And the skirt? Why those?"

"I don't know. I've thought about it a lot and I don't have an answer. Not a good one. Maybe Mom was right, he was under some kind of pressure."

"I just can't picture it. Not Dad."

"I know. It's not exactly the idea of family we grew up with." She snickered. "I certainly don't remember hearing about it in church."

Again Cam tried to imagine his father in the suit, bouncing from the tree. He got the first branch, the thick horizontal one, and the straps tied around it. It was autumn, and the leaves were changing color. They shivered as he bounced, and some dropped off and floated lazily to the ground. He saw that well enough, the shaking of the leaves and the branch, he could even visualize the dark rubber harness. But his father in it, young or old, smiling, sweating, he could not see. He could not get a fix on the man, anymore than he could get a fix on his mother in a tight, sexy swimsuit.

"Cam," Dierdre was saying. "You still there?"

"Yeah," he mumbled. "I guess I should get off."

"You're upset, aren't you?"

"I don't know. Something."

"I used to be. For a long time. It was hard, not just about Dad, but everything. I had to re-think it all. One lie, one secret like that makes you wonder if everything else didn't have some other meaning to it. It makes you doubt your own life."

"Why didn't he just go to some whore? Or have an affair with one of his secretaries?"

"You think that would have been better?"

"It would have been halfway normal."

"He wasn't a bad man, Cam. He did his best. He had problems like the rest of us."

"I wonder what he was thinking all those nights. Waiting for us to go to bed. Waiting until he could get in his little outfit and go outside."

Dierdre didn't reply, and it was some time before Cam realized she was still on the line.

"I gotta go," he said.

"Give it a little time, Cam. It needs time."

"Yeah, sure."

"I'm glad you called. Give my love to Anita and the kids. I'll talk to you soon."

Cam hung up and stared at the wall. On an impulse he picked up the phone and dialed his mother, but hung up after two rings. He wandered to the living room, past the front door. On the floor beneath the mail slot was a pile of letters, one of which was from his mother. He ripped open the envelope with the side of his finger and read the business-like note. Most of it pertained to his father's will. She said that the house seemed very big, which she didn't like, but very much hers, which she did. She mentioned that she'd hired someone, a neighborhood boy, to rake up the leaves in front. She sent her love to Anita and the kids. In a short postscript she wrote that she had gotten rid of the box.

There seemed no reason to keep it, she wrote, *and reason enough to throw it away.*

Cam was not happy. He had intended, he realized, to get the box on his next trip to his mother's. Now it was gone, and he was angry. He felt as though something had been taken from him, something his by right. In what seemed a logical response he decided to make a suit of his own.

He bought a woman's top, with darts of extra material on either side of the zipper in front. He cut the crotch strap and sewed a piece of crinoline around the bottom. He sliced up an old inner tube to make a crude rubber sling, and from what was left cut two or three narrow rubber whips. He already had a pair of boots.

His yard lacked a tree, so Cam decided to use one of the wooden rafters in the garage. One evening when Anita and the kids were visiting friends, he took his box out to the garage and dressed in the suit. He threw the rubber sling over the rafter, tied it, then got in and started bouncing. He was embarrassed at first and felt silly. He tried to think of his father, but nothing would form in his mind. He took up the rubber strips and halfheartedly slapped his thighs and back. It hurt, and after awhile he stopped. He tried bouncing some more, tried to make his mind loose and receptive. Nothing happened. He felt foolish but tried again. Nothing.

After a few minutes he got out of the sling. He unstrapped it and took off the suit, then put everything in the box and went in the house. He was puzzled. He had hoped that the matter would be clearer, but it wasn't. He felt stupid.

He recalled the vision in his mind. Again he saw the maple, its first branch shaking, its red and purple leaves shivering and falling. That was the strongest part of the picture, the tree and the leaves, and it occurred to him that he needed them to make it happen, to make the scene whole. It seemed risky, but he thought he could pull it off.

He spent the next hour planning it out, then wrote his mother a short note saying that he'd like to come up in a week or two to finish the chores. After that he went back to the garage and put the box in the trunk of his car. Then he waited for Anita and the kids to come home.

A week and a half later, on a Saturday, he was at his mother's house. Anita had wanted to join him, but Cam had asked that she allow him to make the trip alone. He made vague references to family matters, and Anita chose not to argue. She could see that he was still trying to get a handle on his father's death.

At his mother's Cam did a day of chores, which included mowing the lawn one last time before winter. He did the front quickly, but in the back he lingered, pausing frequently to look at the maple on the side of the hill. Most of its leaves had fallen, but a few crinkled ones remained. He crept up close, searching the big branch and trunk for some sign of use, a shiny area of bark, a worn spot. There was nothing.

That night at dinner Fran inquired after his family.

"You should have brought them along," she said.

"It's an awfully long drive for the kids," Cam replied. "Just to be here overnight."

"I haven't seen Anita since the memorial."

"She sends her love."

"I like Anita. I've always liked her."

"Yeah. Maybe she'll come next time."

The conversation went slowly, jabbing, skirting, lacking apparent purpose. Eating dinner without his father present seemed to Cam like being on an expedition whose leader had suddenly disappeared. Toward the end of the meal his mother said, awkwardly,

"I'm glad you came, Cam."

He nodded in reply, squashing some food with his fork.

"It gets lonely sometimes. All you kids are gone, and now Jack. I just rattle around."

"It's a big house."

"I have an idea to close off the upper floor. Clean out the bedrooms and keep them empty for you kids to use when you visit. There's enough room down here for me to live in."

"You're not going to sell it?"

"I've thought of it," she said. "It's too soon. I've got other things to tend to first."

"Don't sell it." He looked up from his plate. "I love this house. It doesn't seem right for someone else to live here."

Fran smiled and tears filled her eyes. She wiped them away. "Your coming's a big help, Cam. I know it's not true, but sometimes I feel that I'm in this alone, that I'm the only one suffering Jack's death. At night it's the hardest, in bed. Sometimes I get so full of anxiety and fear that I just freeze up. I'm awake but I can't make my body move, and what's inside just keeps building until I feel like I'm going to shatter. And then suddenly it ends and I can move again and I lie there shaking. It's then I wish Jack were here . . ." She stopped, suddenly embarrassed at sharing this intimacy with her son.

"And then when he's not," she finished quietly, "I think of you children. It calms me to think of you."

Cam sighed, feeling for a moment his mother's loss more than his own. He got up and hugged her, awkwardly, tenderly. He hung by her chair for a minute before sitting down again.

"I miss him too. Sometimes when I least expect it. I'll be sitting around, reading or maybe just looking out the window and all of a sudden it seems like he's there." He paused, remembering. "I expect him to be there, you know what I mean? To tell me what to do."

"That was your father," she said, in a tone that made Cam think suddenly of the bathing suits.

"Are you glad he's dead?"

"Glad? Why would you ask a thing like that?" She was taken aback, momentarily speechless. "I'm not glad, Cam. Relieved a little, I suppose. Your father wasn't an easy man to live with. He thought the world revolved around him and he expected to be looked after. He was a selfish man."

"He loved us. You can't say that he didn't love us."

"Why would I say that? Of course he loved you. He was your father."

"He loved you too."

"In his way."

"He only had his way, Mother. It was the best he could do."

The accusation in his voice hurt her. She tried to think of a reply and ended up leaving the table. Stoicly, she began to clear the dishes. Neither of them spoke. At length Cam went into the living room and turned on the TV. Later, Fran joined him with a cup of tea and some cookies. They ate and watched in silence. It was past eleven when they finally said good night.

Fran went to her bedroom, which sat above the garage. It was attached to the rest of the house by a short book-lined hall. Cam went upstairs to the room he had slept in as a child. He lay restlessly on the bed, half-listening to the radio. An hour went by, and then another. When the announcer said it was half past one, he got up and went downstairs.

His palms were clammy as he slipped nervously out the front door. He wanted this thing to end quickly and without mishap. Briefly, he wondered if his father had felt the same.

He walked to the garage, where he found the door closed. This alarmed him. He didn't dare risk waking his mother by opening it, and after a moment's debate decided to go around to the back. Old and rarely used, the rear door to the garage creaked when he opened it. He slid in quickly and shut it behind him.

He walked behind the Mercedes to his car, which was parked where the boat used to be. He was shaky as he opened the trunk and took out the box. It was a cool evening, and he undressed and dressed quickly. He shut the trunk and put his clothes in the empty box, which he left near the back door. Carrying the sling in one hand and the three rubber whips in the other, he tiptoed outside.

The night had a feeling of early snow in the air. Cam went up the hill to the tree. He dropped the strips of rubber on the ground, unwrapped the sling and threw its ends over the branch. Tying them tight, he picked up the whips and climbed in. Tensely, he began to bounce.

The branch was different than the rafter at home. It moved when he moved, giving a little each time before tugging him back. It was a gentler rhythm, and it worked a kind of hypnotism in him. Gradually his tension eased. He became aware of other things around him. The few remaining leaves rustling at the end of the branch. The cool air on his skin. The tree beside him, and the house, solid, almost human. He looked down at what he was wearing and grinned. The skirt seemed so silly. And the little rubber whips in his hand. He could not possibly use them.

He bounced for awhile more, savoring the night's peace. He stopped when he got tired. He climbed out of the sling and untied it, then went back to the garage. On the way in his foot caught on something. He stumbled against the door. It swung open, creaking loudly, and crashed into the wall behind. He froze, his serenity instantly gone. Sounds came from the room above. A light went on.

Rushing inside, he tore off his clothes. The zipper caught in a piece of crinoline, and he fumbled with it a second before ripping the suit open down the front. He found the box and pulled his clothes out, then dumped everything else inside. Outside a window opened.

"Hello?" he heard his mother say. "Who's out there?"

He put on his shoes without tying them and tucked in his shirt. Then he left the garage, shutting the door behind him.

"It's only me, Mom." He looked up at her window. "Sorry I woke you."

"What are you doing down there? It's two in the morning."

"I couldn't sleep. I needed some fresh air." He started back around the house, while his mother, silhouetted by the light in the bedroom, watched him. He stopped and looked back.

"It's okay, Mom. Go back to bed. I'll see you in the morning."

He disappeared around the corner and ran to the front steps. Once inside, he hurried upstairs, not wanting to meet his mother in the hall. In his room he collapsed on the bed, giddy with relief. He was amazed that he had gone through with it. Nearly being caught had given the whole thing an extra dimension.

He fell asleep on top of the bed. The radio played all night. He woke in the morning feeling rested, even though he had only slept a few hours. He washed and went downstairs to the kitchen. His mother wasn't there, but there was a hot pot of coffee sitting in the Mr. Coffee machine. He poured himself a cup and went out to the front porch to see what kind of day it was. It was cold and clear; a thin frost lay on the lawn. He hugged the coffee cup with his hands and let the steam warm his face. He felt surprisingly good.

He wandered down the front steps, appreciating the peace of the house and the neighborhood. When he got to the driveway, he noticed that the Mercedes had been pulled out of the garage. The door was still open, and he walked in, expecting to see his mother. She wasn't there. He was about to turn back when he saw the box. It was sitting where he had left it, not far from the rear door. With the Mercedes out of the way it stood out like a confession.

Cam stared, the breath sticking in his chest as it had the night before when the door had slammed into the wall. He looked around to be sure he was alone, then went over to it. It looked the same as before, but he couldn't remember exactly how he had left it. The flaps were closed . . . had he done that? He had a feeling the box was turned in a different direction and stepped back to visualize it. He shut his eyes and tried to put together each detail of the night before, but the more he tried the more uncertain he got. He looked again. He couldn't tell. With each passing moment his memory seemed to change.

Disgusted with himself and worried, he grabbed the box and threw it angrily in the trunk of his car. The calm of the morning was gone. He tried to convince himself there was nothing to be ashamed of, but he couldn't make it work. He felt open to attack and frantically sought a plausible explanation to give his mother. What would his father have said? He pressed his hands to his temples and closed his eyes in concentration.

"Is something the matter?"

He was startled. "No," he said, recovering quickly as his mother entered the garage. "I was just thinking."

"You were up late."

"Yeah. I guess I'm a little tired." He stretched, avoiding her eyes.

"I've made some breakfast," she said. "You should have something to eat before you go."

He started out of the garage, then stopped. "How come you got the Mercedes out?"

"I'm going to church. Why?"

"Nothing," he muttered.

She gave him a look. "Cam, are you all right?"

"I'm fine."

On the way to the house he kept trying to catch a glimpse of her eyes without looking at her. In the kitchen, by her attitude he was sure that she knew. Five minutes later, as he finished his eggs and toast, he was just as sure that she didn't. He cleared the dishes, while his mother sat back, nursing a cup of coffee.

"I'm glad you came, Cam. It helps. It helps to know there's family."

"Yeah," he said, smiling feebly. "I'm glad too."

She gave him a look of unmarred affection and love. Then her face became solemn.

"What's the matter," he asked anxiously.

She stared into her cup, slowly swirling the grounds. "It's been a hard time, hasn't it?"

He nodded, his heart racing. Fran looked up.

"It'll pass, won't it? This feeling of uncertainty. Of unreality."

With an effort Cam met her eyes, looking for a sign, some kind of acknowledgment. He found nothing, and realized suddenly that he might never know. Discretion was his mother's consummate skill; protecting her son from shame would be a measure of her love. He was unexpectedly touched.

"It'll pass," he said, going to her, cradling her head. "It takes time."

She rested wordlessly in his hands. At length she looked at her watch. It was time for church.

"I had better be going," she said, pushing her chair out from the table. "It's best not to be late."

She left the room and Cam went upstairs to get his things. By the time she came out the front door, he was already in his car, warming the engine. She came over to him, buttoning her wool coat on the way. He got out, and they hugged and kissed goodbye. He got back in, stared out the window a moment, then got out and hugged her again. Then he climbed back in, put the car in gear and drove off.

Fran went to the Mercedes and started it up. She pushed a button and the garage door came down. The sun had begun to melt the frost on the lawn. When the Mercedes was warm, she drove to church.

THE THING ITSELF

To Hetty

This is a story about love. It is about Laurie and Elliot, two people who meet in their late twenties. Laurie is a nurse and an outdoorswoman. She jogs and she hikes. She has had experiences with men, none of them long. She prefers her enlistments short and definable.

Elliot is a doctor. He has cystic fibrosis, a disease of the lungs and pancreas. He is a dedicated and conscientious worker and a wit. A vivid imagination is his handle on survival.

There are lessons in this story. Particular ones, and universal. A video is forthcoming. And later, a syndicated column. Love, after all, is not so hard. It is not a city, or a thought. When attended to with foresight and maturity, love is as straightforward as boiling an egg.

I. The Roll of the Dice

Laurie met Elliot while she was working in the intensive care unit. It was in the early morning hours after the fire that had swept through the college women's dormitory, and all medical personnel had been mobilized. The blackened bodies of coeds hadn't yet been removed from the crowded corridors. They lined the walls, silent lumps under crumpled white sheets. The smell was horrible. Families raged and grieved, while nurses, doctors,

145

administrators, orderlies performed their grim tasks. The proportions of the tragedy stripped away artifice. The normally meticulous women forgot about their makeup, their lipstick and eyeliner. Mascara trickled in tears down their cheeks. The carefully-groomed administrators had no time to shave, and tiny splinters of hair stuck out from their chins and cheeks. For a short while these people came together in a way unknown to them by the light of bright and ordered day.

Laurie found Elliot in the ICU. They had communicated several times before under purely routine circumstances. The lids of his eyes seemed to close as he leaned over the girl in the bed. He placed his stethoscope on her chest, and shook his head.

"Take a break," Laurie said. "You've been here all night."

Elliot pretended not to hear. His forehead was nearly touching the singed skin of the girl. He tried to hold back his tears.

Laurie stood silently next to the bed. Her stethoscope was draped over her neck, her hands squeezed the side rail. She watched Elliot, who seemed so sad and alive. She reached across the dying girl and took his hand.

"C'mon, let's have a cup of coffee."

Elliot let her lead him to the nurse's lounge, where they sat on a cheap plastic couch. It was split down the middle, and the foam showed through. Elliot held his face in his hands, staring at the floor. Laurie bent the spigot of the coffee machine, filling two cups with lukewarm coffee. Her eyes were bloodshot; the gray bags beneath them made her look twice her age. She had been a nurse for five years, and this had been the worst night of her life. Unconsciously, she put her hand on Elliot's neck and began to rub.

Elliot let her, not expecting to relax. He was too tired to sleep. He put the coffee cup on the table and touched Laurie's leg. He turned sideways on the couch, crossed his legs in a yoga position and stretched out his back. Laurie rubbed it. She leaned closer and pulled him against her. Snaking her hands between the buttons at the front of his shirt, she touched his chest.

Elliot took her to the on-call room and locked the door. He made a few lame jokes about doctors and nurses. She laughed a little too loud. When they made love, it was slow then very quick. Elliot was funny and gentle. Laurie was surprised at how easy it was. She got hot fast and reached a sharp climax. Elliot came too, and in moments was asleep. His breathing was rapid and coarse for a long time. Laurie stayed awake. She was amazed. A verse from somewhere played in her mind:

> *The dead come knocking*
> *The dead come knocking*
> *And love, sweet love,*
> *It lets them in.*

II. Choosing the Right Species

Tall men aroused in Laurie feelings she preferred to avoid. She was five foot three, and Elliot, if anything, was half an inch shorter. This suited Laurie just fine. When they moved in together, they kept things — books, pots, linen — close to the ground. They left the top shelves in the kitchen empty, and made sure their two full length mirrors were hung low on the doors.

A month after getting the apartment, Elliot came down with pneumonia. He was put in the hospital and ended up staying for three weeks. During this time Laurie got a taste of a different life. She visited him daily, twice when she could. They did crosswords together, read to each other, shared meals. Elliot craved starches — noodles and spaghetti — because of his body's poor ability to digest protein. Laurie brought in food and ate with him. She got a little fat. She stopped jogging because she didn't have time, and saw more of his nurses than her own friends.

On the whole, though, she was happy. She had a man, and the man loved her. He needed her. It made her feel good.

Elliot's pneumonia slowly improved. His breathing became easier, and the oxygen was taken away. Soon he was able to say more than one or two sentences without getting out of breath.

"Imagination," he told Laurie, "is the source of my strength. When I stop inventing, I will die."

He was twenty-nine, and had already lived years beyond others with his disease. His future was not bright.

"Fiction is power," he went on. "Out of it grows fact. Avoidance is sometimes more direct than study."

Elliot loved the sound of words and the shelter they brought. When he had the breath, he could talk for hours. He told Laurie stories.

One day they were lying together in his hospital bed, Elliot in his issued gown, Laurie in a skirt and blouse. The nurses allowed the intimacy because Laurie was one of them, because Elliot was a doctor. They allowed it because they were sympathetic; they understood the nature of health and recovery.

The back of the bed was raised so that Elliot could breathe easier. Laurie was nestled by his side, one hand draped across his stomach. She was half-asleep, timing her breathing to the cadence of Elliot's voice.

"Like the Pope," he was saying, "I believe in angels. Not good and bad ones, as he supposes. Reflective ones. Mirrors in the shapes of möbius strips. A kind of personal and mathematical afterlife. Are you listening?"

She nodded sleepily.

"It is not simply belief," he went on. "There are certain proofs . . ." He paused, looking down at the her hand on his belly. It was finely-veined, strong, and the arm, the soft belly of the biceps was beautiful as it disappeared into the sleeve of her blouse. He became aware of her breasts pressed against his side.

"There is a restaurant," he said. "I have visited it more than once. Its atmosphere is unique; its elegance, legendary. The special there is an ambrosial delight not to be found elsewhere. Not were you to search a lifetime." He put a hand on her breast and spoke authoritatively. "Mother's milk. Not milk and honey, nor the milk of human kindness, not even the milky tears of dew at dawn. Simply, purely, pleasingly, Mother's milk. The brew of Mammalia. The sustenance of our kind."

She smiled dreamily. Encouraged, Elliot went on.

"Here," he swept out an arm, "on our very premises we house a wide variety of creatures. The multitudinous reflections of God's eye are yours to choose from. In cages in the basement we have rabbit, chipmunk, gopher and beaver. Our shrew milk is heavenly, though scant. An agile child has been trained to gather it: her tiny, supple fingers deftly milk the precious fluid into thimbles, which you may purchase as souvenirs.

"In a corral adjoining the flank of the restaurant lie our marsupials, the wombats and koalas, the kangaroos. Beyond, in our rolling grasslands, dotted with oak and madrone, irrigated by fifteen miles of flexible conduit, waters from artesian wells, graze elephant, ass, moose, zebra, yak, giraffe and llama. Anteaters forage there, and armadillos. It is still summer, and the young of these creatures are not yet weaned. There is milk in abundance, thick milk, thin, sweet and bitter. Some is white as snow, some yellow, other gray as ash. We have a team of starving children, adept at identification, trained to run quickly and carefully. They keep low, and draw upon udders with acrobatic skill and finesse. For each cup of milk delivered to our kitchen they receive a handful of coin; every third cup nets them a day of rest. They are strong-hearted and eager to please. Choose your mammal and feed a child."

He paused to gather his breath. Laurie yawned, stretched. "You haven't mentioned the carnivores," she said.

"We offer a complete listing. The cost, as you might expect, is higher. The risks are greater, the mothers not so obliging. Extraction is more labor-intensive, requiring from two to five brave souls. We don't use tranquilizer guns, as it would taint the milk. A mothering carnivore, be it badger, weasel, lion, bear or wolf is a touchy animal. Her glands are guarded items, the product a precious commodity. But a sip of cheetah milk . . ." He sighed, licking his lips, "it puts hair on your chest."

"I don't need more hair," said Laurie. She touched a scratch mark on her calf. "I have to shave too much as it is, and I hate it."

"Then you should definitely skip the carnivores. Besides, the milk has a tendency to be harsh. Causes the mouth to pucker." He pursed his lips and blew her a kiss.

"Ethical considerations require that the last class go unnamed. Strictly speaking, we are not even supposed to have the milk available. Gathering it has been declared an objectification of the provider. Many who are not in need of the income consider it degrading. Others claim that its collection and availability carry sexual overtones that should not be confused with food. Notwithstanding these objections, it is a most popular item."

"Men, I presume, favor it more than women."

"Surprisingly not. Women choose it as often."

"It's in your mind, Elliot."

He laughed. "I'm a piece of fiction."

"You're a good man. What will I do without you?"

"Don't be maudlin." He started to say more but was interrupted by the beginnings of a cough. It started deep in his chest and rumbled up like thunder. His face suffused with blood, and his whole body shook. It seemed like he was tearing his insides out.

"Should I call the nurse?"

He didn't answer, working his lungs until finally he brought something up. He spit it into some Kleenex, then reached over and turned on the oxygen. He stuck the plastic prongs in his nose.

Laurie watched. She waited. Her initial apprehension gradually faded, but a knot of tension stayed in her stomach. She was still learning this man's routine. This life.

"I'm worried about you," she said at length.

"It's okay," he said, panting. His forehead was beaded with sweat. "I . . . have to . . . get . . . the phlegm up."

"It's always like this?"

He nodded. They held hands and listened to the oxygen bubbling quietly up beside the bed. Gradually his breathing calmed. Laurie asked him about dying.

"Everyone dies," he said.

"But you have CF."

"I don't think about it. Only when I'm sick."

She looked at him quizzically. "I don't believe you."

He stared at her, then looked away. "I think about it. What's the difference?"

"The difference is I'm involved. I just found you. I don't want you to die."

"I won't die."

She was not convinced.

"I won't," he repeated. "I promise. Listen . . ." He took her hand. "There's one more item. One more kind of milk."

"Stop," she said.

"No. Listen. It's the last. The purest. It's a vapor, it enters through closed lips, condenses on the tongue. It's the sweetest milk there is. Full of gentleness and comfort. The breath of an angel."

"I don't believe in angels," she said stiffly. "This is about dying, isn't it?" Tears brimmed her eyes. "You're going to die, aren't you?"

"No." He shook his head. "It's just a story."

III. Imagination and Good Health

Love requires health. Health is hypnotism, trust, science. It is persuasion and power, belief spread like a blanket, a bed. It is rational, irrational. Chemistry, words, light and sound.

An agent can be employed. A drug, for example, a root. Or a shell, mud, bark, the husk of an insect. A scalpel can be the agent. The ace of cups. There are capsules the size of cherries, poultices that smell like tar. Horn of goat, spore of fungus, fender, headlight, bottlecap. A healer must not be narrow-minded.

He can tell a story.

Elliot is a healer, a doctor of medicine. He works in a windowless room with a desk and a table. A curtain can be drawn
around the table for privacy. Patients who willingly lie naked for
his examination use the curtain's screen to re-clothe themselves. It
is the shield behind which they recover their dignity.

On the wall above his desk is taped a card with the words Do
No Harm. Out of sight on the back is a quote from a friend: I've
always said I don't mind nobody bullshitin' me, but if you're going
to jive make it good. Make me believe it.

One afternoon a woman enters his office. She is overweight
and wears pants whose zipper is broken. She has a loose-fitting
t-shirt and a bandanna that hides her hair. Settling in the chair
beside his desk, she says, "I got burning."

Elliot is tired from a bad night. He stifles a yawn. "Burning?"

"All up in my head," she touches it, "and down my back. It
draws on me. Cuts clear from back to front. My arms and legs
too. My whole body burns."

Elliot thumbs through her chart, thick with multiple visits,
multiple complaints. Even before knowing what she has, he won-
ders what she wants.

"How long have you had the burning?"

The woman calculates. "Two days, maybe three."

"Have you tried anything?"

"Rubbing alcohol."

He nods.

"Listerine."

He waits for more, but the woman is close-lipped. She stares
in her lap, as though awaiting punishment.

"And did they help?"

"They soothed a little. I still got the burning."

Elliot is drowsy, and his mind is not working well. Burning
makes him think of sparks, fire, sexual yearning. He knows if he
is not careful, the thread will vanish and he will lose control.

He tells her to undress, and when she is ready he goes to
examine her. She does not appear ill. In the midst of listening to

her lungs, Elliot is struck by a fit of coughing. He retreats across the room, leaning against his desk until the paroxysm passes. Winded and slightly embarrassed, he completes the exam. He draws the curtain and tells her to dress.

At his desk he ponders his own health. It is slowly failing. He feels it when he tries a deep breath. Always he wants for air.

The woman seems healthy enough. He resents this, but also he is grateful. Her story is making him work and forget. When she is dressed and sitting, he has a sense again of her fear.

"The exam," he says carefully, "is normal."

"Then what's the burning?"

"It's a reaction to something. Maybe a virus. Or an allergy. It should be gone in a few days."

She looks at him, her face working to stay calm. Her eyes are everywhere but at his. "My mother died of cancer."

"This is not cancer."

"It ate her up. In the end the fever got her. Burned her till she couldn't eat. Couldn't breathe either."

"You do not have cancer." Elliot takes her by the wrist and forces her to look at him. "Do you understand?"

"I'm not going to die?"

"Not of this."

"Are you sure?"

"Listen to me. This is not cancer. You are not going to die."

She looks away, and then her eyes dart back, as if to make sure he is telling the truth.

"You believe me?"

She nods tentatively, then stands. "I feel better. The burning, it'll go away?"

"Yes. Call me next week."

She leaves, and Elliot settles in his chair. He feels charged by the encounter. On a scrap of paper he scribbles the words "science: to know," and beneath them, "fiction: to shape." Next to "fiction" he sketches a picture of a syringe and needle. He draws a colony of bacteria and an equation to estimate the blood flow through the heart. Above it, opposite the word "science", he sketches the face of a man. He has a single eye, from whose pupil radiate tiny stars, half-moons, mythical animals in miniature. They rise above his head, where they circle in a cloud of barely discernible shapes. They look like the bacteria below, and noting this, Elliot draws a bridge connecting the two. He smiles, then yawns. He is tired. Cradling his arms on the desktop, he puts his head down.

Sometime later, a knock on the door stirs him. Heavy-lidded and still half-asleep, he swivels in his chair. Through the door walks a clown in full regalia — whiteface, painted smile, pink wig. On his forehead is penciled a blue eye.

Elliot stares. He rubs his eyes. There is another knock, and he turns to the door, grateful for the interruption. This time a skeleton hobbles in, all bones, ambulating without visible means of support. In its teeth is clenched a cigar, whose smoke trails up and hangs in its eye sockets. The skeleton takes a position near the clown, who regards Elliot with a gay, fixed smile. He wrinkles his forehead, and the eye there blinks.

Elliot is speechless. His mind skirts over the day's events, searching for clues. Did he eat something bad? Was there a drug in his morning tea? Something in the air? The skeleton and clown seem to be waiting. There is another sound at the door, followed by a brief inrush of air. Elliot girds himself and turns. Standing in the doorway is a naked man, his face and torso vaguely familiar. Sweeping out from his back are wings.

Elliot numbly watches this last one enter, then gets up and shuts the door. This is a private matter, he is sure. It occurs to him that it might be his time to die.

The three gaze at him without detectable emotion. The clown speaks.

"Life is not simple, my friend. You've probably noticed. Boundaries constantly change. It is a difficult concept for the egocentric mind.

"A person, for example, starts as a single cell. The cell divides, migrates, differentiates. There is no 'fact' of existence."

"Who are you?" Elliot asks. His voice is shaky.

"Nor of non-existence," the winged person continues. "Dead tissue is carried off by scavengers. Bones, by droplets of water. Death is hardly less complicated."

"Why are you here? Who are you?"

"There is no thing that does not change. There is no fact. There is only fiction."

"We are Humor, Death, Science," says the clown. "Your homunculi. A lovely triad, don't you think?"

"Think?" Elliot stammers. "Am I thinking?"

"Don't be cute." The skeleton waves its cigar. "I was told you were a nice fellow."

"Courteous," says the clown.

"Kind."

"Why are you here?" Elliot asks.

"A lesson in geography," rattles the skeleton. "Boundaries. The imagination."

"You scare me."

"We could not possibly harm you," murmurs the one with wings.

"There is, however, the question of health." The clown scribbles a formula in the air. "Science is chemistry. Sub-atomics is the nature of things."

"The end of things is the nature of things," says the skeleton. "Forgetfulness is such a blessing."

"The wind is a blessing," says the winged one. Of the three he seems the most human. "Breath is the common origin. It is the source of inspiration."

"Which of the triad are you?" Elliot asks.

"I am Death," whispers the angel.

Elliot is now visibly shaken. He strains to think of something to say, to do. The tension rises in his body. When it hits his chest, he is seized by a fit of coughing. It is a bad one, lasting more than a minute. By the time it ends, he is breathless. His face is red, his head between his legs.

"Air," he whispers. "Air."

IV. Doing Things Together

At the foot of Elliot and Laurie's bed is a twenty-four inch Sony color television. The remote control device lies between them on the sheet. They are watching the Miss America Beauty Pageant.

Elliot is bored with the contestants, putting up with their dime store, egregious obsequies in order to catch a glimpse of the true star, the enigmatic Bert Parks. Parks is a kind of hero to Elliot. He seems to age so gracelessly, like no man on earth, from the lizard-like skin at his neck to the sleazy, hungry and haunted pits that pass for his eyes. His smile is a lurid caricature, evoking death camp assurances and promises. And his singing . . . his singing is mesmerizing.

A rhapsody to the beatific pucker of femininity, Parks' voice is a tribute to science. To mind over matter, imagination over true flesh. When Parks sings, Elliot nearly weeps. He thinks of drugs stronger than morphine, of direct stimulation of the neural centers of pain and pleasure. He is astounded by the man, by his determination, his self-denigration, his longevity. During the closing bars of the pageant's hymn, Elliot suddenly realizes that Parks is not human.

If he studies the man's image carefully, he can discern gaps between body parts. When one of the contestants passes behind him, Elliot catches a glimpse of the sequins on her dress through Parks' thyroid gland. When Parks turns to greet her, pink feathers (presumably from her head piece) sprout from his eye sockets. It is a revelation. Bert Parks, the suave, polished, unctuous ringmaster is an illusion.

Laurie is more interested in the girls. She is captivated by their glossy smiles and precise bodies. Their perfect nails and hair, and endless legs. Despite her humiliation at their grating optimism and choreographed gaiety, Laurie is envious. She imagines futures of attention and worth, of great personal magnetism and reward. She feels inadequate. Taking the remote control device in a hand, she punches off the TV.

"Am I pretty?" she says to Elliot.

"Exceptionally."

"No. Don't answer fast. I want you to think about it. I want the truth."

He cups his chin in his palm and looks her over. The wide, acne-pocked forehead. Weak chin, full breasts, short, fat legs.

"You are beautiful," he says.

She looks him in the eye. "You mean it?"

"I mean it. Beautiful. It's as simple as that."

Laurie smiles then, a broad, teary-eyed smile. "I love you, Elliot. If I could, I'd give you my breath. I'd breathe for you."

"Laurie," he says, taking her hands, "if I could, I'd sing for you. I'd sing words that you'd believe, and I'd put them in your brain in a place you'd never forget . . ." He pauses, then laughs.

"If I could, Laurie, I'd be Bert Parks for you. I'd be immortal."

V. Working It Out

Laurie works in the intensive care unit. Sometimes it is slow, sometimes busy. Of the six beds in the unit only one is filled tonight. In it is a thirty-year-old man who looks ninety. His eyes are yellow, his arms spindly, his face sallow. His belly is so swollen that he has not seen his feet in months. He can't lie flat because it is impossible to breathe, so he has to be propped up in bed. He doesn't sleep well but can't take pills because his liver is shot. He has terminal cirrhosis and has been in and out of a coma for days.

Presently he is in, which means that there is not much for Laurie to do. From time to time she checks his bottles, and every hour she takes his vital signs. Between these small tasks she sits at the nurse's station reading an outdoor magazine. Tonight she finds it boring, and keeps reading the same passage over and over. She is thinking about Elliot.

All her life Laurie has depended on men. This she resents, and so for years has made a deal with herself. A secret, barely conscious deal: her men will have flaws. Her first lover was unreliable; her second, distant and moody. The one before Elliot indulged himself in a cause more than he did in Laurie. Elliot's flaw is his illness. It puts the two of them, she feels, on equal footing. He cannot leave her because he needs her. He depends on her. This gives her a sense of security. It makes her feel curiously independent and strong. She has casually forgotten the inevitability of his early death. She is unaware of how carefully she has chosen a situation that will soon cause her grief. Laurie herself lives in a world of periodic coma.

She has a cup of coffee, and then another. Between three and five are the worst hours of the morning, the hardest to stay awake. She starts to do her nails but stops because she doesn't really care. The girls are girls; she is a woman. The men can meet her on her own ground.

The coffee has its effect, and her head begins to buzz. Her hands get jittery, and she starts to have a few wild thoughts. From the bed of the cirrhotic she hears a sound. There is a curtain around him, and when she gets up to look behind it, he is gone. In his place is a man with wings.

Oh shit, Laurie thinks. Something's wrong. Something's terribly wrong. Then the nurse in her takes over.

She makes the man comfortable, fluffing up the pillow and straightening the sheets. His wings curl around, resting on his torso and upper thighs. He smiles up at her from a drawn face: he does not look well at all. She gives him a sip of water, and he thanks her with his eyes. She tells herself that she should report this to her supervisor, but as she turns to go, he touches her with a wing. He makes her understand that he wants her to take a feather. As a gift. A token. Laurie refuses, but the man insists. It is all so very strange.

Finally she consents, choosing a small white primary near the tip. She tugs on it, but it sticks tight. She pulls harder, and harder still.

It comes loose with a pop, then a hiss. Laurie feels a soft stream of air against her face. It tastes faintly of milk.

She touches her lips with the tip of the feather. The hiss continues. She realizes she has acted willfully. It does not surprise her. All things must pass. She is a survivor. The man's time is up.

VI. Song and Lament

You promised you wouldn't die. You said it, and yet you bought life insurance every chance you got. At eighteen, twenty, twenty-five. Twenty-five years old! There is no insurance at twenty-five, at twenty-five some people open their eyes for the first time. Open them and see a world. Take the wrong turn sometimes, stumble maybe, but none would call it death. Disappointment, sure. A setback. But not death. How can we die before we even open our eyes?

But it was different for you. You were sick from the start. Your mother said she wouldn't have had you if she'd known. She was crying when she said that, it was after you died. She would have aborted, she said, if not with the help of someone with conscience, then in some back alley. With a stick, a hanger. With lye if she had to. However dangerous and terrible, she would have tried. Because life was too hard for you. Too damned hard.

You couldn't run or skip, couldn't move fast to save your life. Couldn't scale a peak and stand above the world, stretch out where there's nothing but sky. Or pause on an alpine trail, lupine clumped around the base of a gnarled juniper, wind in your face, snow in the air. Stop and sit on a piece of granite the size of an elephant. Share lunch. You couldn't breathe the mountain air, the fine, crystalline air. The oxygen was too thin, your lungs too choked with phlegm. You almost died when we drove across the Rockies.

But you said dying wasn't on your mind when you weren't sick. When you weren't laid out in bed, coughing, panting, struggling to bring up the phlegm. You said you didn't think about it, but how could you not? How could you not be afraid the next day might be just a little harder, your lungs more tired, your breath feebler. When you're sick like that, isn't every day a sick day, even when you're better? Don't the pills get old, and the treatments? Isn't there a part of you that waits for things to worsen, that expects to die?

But you said no, and showered me with fancy words and stories. With gentleness and patience. With love.

Sometimes you seemed a saint. Tough, vulnerable. Weakened, you were stronger. Resilient. Erotic.

You were the sexiest man I knew.

You didn't hike, or swim. Didn't cook. You talked to me. You listened. You made jokes and made love.

You used to come home after work—after ten, twelve exhausting hours at the hospital—and boil a package of spaghetti for dinner. Spaghetti and butter. That was it. For dinner. No wonder you died.

You made me laugh, see? Taught me humor. Imagination. Things to ease the pain.

Like buying that guidebook of San Francisco with each street labeled according to its grade. Red was steep, yellow gentle, blue level. You plotted a course through the city, convinced me the modest hills were mountain peaks, the brightly-painted victorians sweet-smelling pine. Stray cats were skunk, dogs were wolf and deer. The reservoirs were alpine lakes, and you carried repellent to keep the mosquitoes down.

You were good at easing the pain, Elliot. The pain of less. The pain of having to lose you.

I remember the last morphine shot, the one that let you lie back, that let the knotted muscles in your chest and neck finally

ease. The room was dark, your friends circled the bed like a
hand. One by one they told the stories, they made a web of mem-
ories with you at the center. So that when they were done, you
were remembered, and free to go. You slumped against me, heavy,
loose at last, and asked, Can I die. Your voice was so feeble I
scarcely heard. Can I die?

Yes, I whispered. Yes, yes, die now.

You smiled, and your mouth got slack. You gave a little shud-
der, and you died.

I did not weep. I felt anger and sadness. Your weight. I
watched the moonlight on the floor. I heard wheels in the hall.
The world had wings.

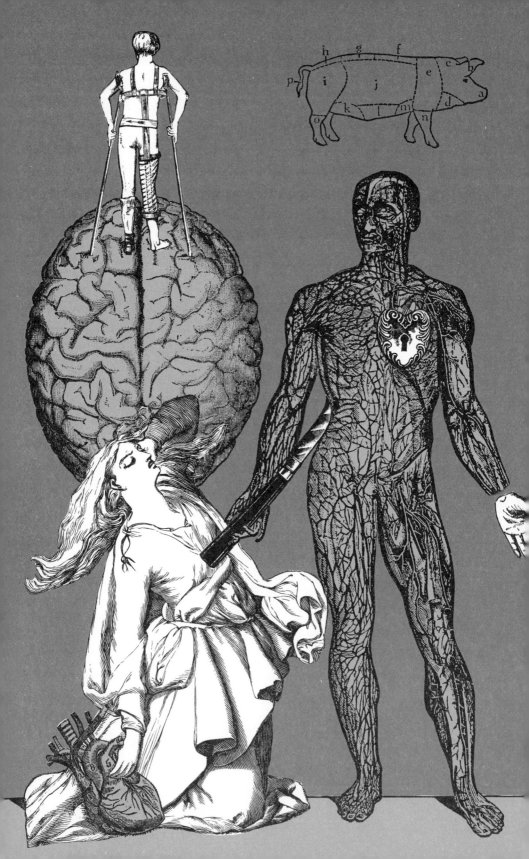

BESTSELLER

October 20

I once believed that poverty was a desirable state, a way for an artist to focus his mind, to distinguish the inessential from the essential. I was younger then and needed less. A simple room with a bed, a chair, a table. An old typewriter, some pencils, a stack of cheap paper. I prided myself on my economies, even though I could easily have found a job and lived otherwise. Asceticism seemed the proper breeding ground for a writer.

Things are different now. I have a family, and while poverty may serve some obscure personal purpose, I cannot accept it for my wife and son. They deserve better than recycled clothes and a tiny, dank apartment. Potato soup and week-old vegetables. Better than to hear me beg our landlord for a rent extension, or come home to a frigid apartment because the heat's been cut off. Indigence is no achievement.

I hate being poor.

October 21

Had a tough time with the book today. Dialogue felt flat, characters like they'd been collectively drugged. In the middle of asking myself what sense it meant to write something that didn't even hold my own interest, Tony called with the news that paperback rights to *In the Thicket* had been sold, but for only a fraction of what we'd hoped. And *Ordeal on the Neighbor's Lawn* has been re-maindered. No big surprise but enough to put an end to today's work. Tony gently asked about the new book, and I answered in vague but enthusiastic terms. "Commercial potential" were, I think, the words I used. They sounded less threatening coming from me than Tony, but after we hung up, their meaning seemed as baffling as ever. What the hell do I have to do to write a book that sells?

October 23

Nick goes through clothes like they were made of paper. Seems like every few days we're either patching something or making a trip to the Salvation Army. He's needed a new pair of shoes for a month now. I told him how Charlie Chaplin used a piece of bologna to patch a hole in his shoe in *Modern Times*. Nickie was intrigued.

"Where'd he get it?"

"From walking."

He looked at me, and I could see him thinking it through. "No," he said. "Where'd he get the bologna?"

October 27

After a week of toothache that wouldn't quit, Claire broke down and went to the dentist. The guy wanted to do a root canal and put in some kind of bridge. Four hundred bucks. Claire told him to pull it. I was furious.

"I can't believe you let him do that. It's your body, Claire. Teeth don't grow back."

"I'm not stupid," she said.

"I can't believe it. Four hundred bucks. Did you tell the ass-hole we don't have that kind of money?"

"That's enough, Matt."

"Did you?"

"Matt," she said, stopping me with one of her looks. "I've got plenty left."

It's hard to stay mad at a woman like Claire. That look of hers is a killer. To tell the truth, she's kind of cute with a gap in the middle of her smile.

October 29

Took Nick to the park after school, watched while he climbed the big cypress back of the tennis court. He's such a beauty, that boy. Nimble, fearless, reminded me of my own childhood, climbing like that. Young and invincible, one branch after another to the top of the tree. All sky up there. King of the world.

And even that time I fell, stepped on air instead of branch and plummeted twenty feet to the ground, even then something magical. Stunned, my rib cage vibrating like a string, I wandered though the forest in a trance. Finally made it home, bearing a lesson. The earth does not move when I strike it. Some things do not yield to my will.

Nick waved from the top of the cypress, and I caught myself praying he did not have to fall, hoping there was some other, easier way to learn.

On the way home he kept lagging behind. Said that his leg hurt. Damn shoes, they probably got hung up on one of the branches. I swore to Nick we'd get a new pair as soon as a check comes.

November 1

Claire called from work in a state. They doubled the number of calls she has to take per hour, which of course makes the callers even angrier than they were to begin with. I took a break from the book and met her for lunch. She was nearly in tears.

"Some of the people are so rude. Over a goddamned dishwasher or some stupid toaster-oven. Like their machine is more important than I am."

"Quit," I told her.

"This woman called today to complain that her husband's shirts weren't getting white enough. He's mad at her because he doesn't have a clean shirt to wear to work. So she calls and gets mad at me. Can you believe it?"

"What did you say to her?"

"I went through the whole routine, but she didn't want to hear. She just wanted to be mad. I don't need it."

"Everyone's mad," I said. "Quit."

"Don't keep saying that."

"You hate it."

"What I hate is when you make things sound so simple. It's like you're trying to fool me. You're telling a lie."

"It's no lie, Claire."

She looked away. "I'm not in the mood for this."

"Other people are just like us. They want their lives to live up to their dreams. They're trying to find a little hope."

"I can't believe yelling at me possibly helps." She shook her head and grumbled, eventually dismissing the subject with a disgruntled sigh.

"Did you work today?"

"It was like pulling teeth, if you'll excuse the expression."

She didn't smile. "Has Tony seen any of it?"

"A couple of chapters. He thinks we can make some money. At least as much as *Thicket*."

"Not exactly a rousing endorsement."

"Forget Tony. We'll make money. If we don't, I'll find another way."

"Sure you would."

"I mean it."

She regarded me queerly, then took out her compact and freshened her lips. After she'd gone, I stayed at the table, thinking over what I'd said. As a boy the possibilities of success abounded, but as an adult that same world seems far more difficult to locate. Nevertheless, my ambition remains fierce. This worries me sometimes. Am I lying to myself, as Claire seems to think? Could I ever truly give up writing?

November 4

Up day today. Words flew onto the page in a fury. Finished Chapter Eleven, and for the first time everything seems in place. Jaime's beginning to come around . . . by the end he will have redeemed himself. The marriage of hope to sadness, it'll be a fitting conclusion. And just the kind of thing that'll sell.

November 5

Nick complains about his leg. Still tender where he fell, and he limps ever so slightly. Funny, when I was a kid, seems like I recovered from bumps and bruises overnight. Maybe it's just growing pains. Anyway, I gave him a couple of aspirin, which seemed to help. If he's not better by the time Claire gets her paycheck, I'll take him to the doctor.

November 8

During a lull in the writing found myself looking through the want-ads. All sorts of job opportunities and the accompanying visions of wealth. I let myself go, imagining the great adventures I could have as a filing clerk, memorizing long series of numbers, breathing paper dust and filing one folder after another. Or as a loan processor, recipient of all the hope and loathing people extend onto agents of finance. A cook perhaps, knowing as I do the masterly craft of opening cans and heating their contents. Or a secretary, typing with clumsy fingers and answering the phone with cloaked civility. There was an opening for a librarian that sounded appealing, and on a whim I dialed the number. The woman, though pleasant, was unimpressed by the fact that I was a published author. In fact, in some subtle way she seemed to hold it against me, as though I would be the last person on earth capable of helping a reader. When she discovered I lacked the proper college degree, she advised me not to apply for the job and hung up. Her rejection upset me, and I quickly dialed another number, choosing an advertisement at random just to prove that I was at least capable of getting past a phone call. A man came on the line and when I told him I was interested in a job, he asked if I had experience with the DBX 2000, the TAC 143, the QT 1522 and the BRT 6200. After a slight pause I told him yes, I did have some knowledge of car engines, having worked extensively on my old Toyota before it blew a head gasket and died a year ago. There was a brief silence on his end of the line, and then he said he wasn't looking for jokers and hung up.

I was deflated, feeling in some strange way that my manhood had been insulted. With unexpected determination I searched the ads for anything to assuage my injured pride. Past dental assistants, escorts and car salesmen. Machinists, cosmetic counterpersons, TV repairmen. Each more implausible than the last, and I was about to give up when my eyes caught a box at the bottom of the page. "DONORS NEEDED," it read. "Good health the only requirement."

I called the number, and the most delightful woman answered. She represented a medical organization that was conducting a study, and if I were in good health she would be happy to set up an appointment for an interview. Under further questioning, she explained that their research was in the field of organ transplantation, though she was quick to reassure me that the study required only a questionnaire and simple blood test. They were offering two hundred dollars to all those who enrolled. She concluded by saying, rather cryptically, that under the right circumstances there was the opportunity for lucrative, full-time employment.

Her persuasiveness was such that I was about to make an appointment, when I realized that I had never really intended to go through with any of this. My whim had taken me farther than I intended.

Thanking her, I hung up, disturbed at how close I had been to substituting some other project for the book. There's no question that money's tight, but we'll get by. The book will be finished before long, and once it sells we'll get out of this rat-trap life for good.

November 9

Walked down by the wharf this afternoon, reconstituting after a rough morning. The sharp, briny smell of salt water and fish was a tonic. The one-armed man at Scoma's, the big Italian with the crooked nose was dumping palletfuls of crab into his chest-high vat of boiling water. Fat, pink claws, severed from their bodies, floated to the surface.

I started to order one for dinner, then stopped when I realized the price. Instead, I bought a bag of fish guts and a couple of old heads. Thinking soup but I couldn't bring myself to it. Ended up feeding the slop to some seals, who barked and clapped their flippers appreciatively.

On the way home I passed a quadriplegic woman playing piano with her tongue. A newspaper clipping tacked on a board behind her told how she was a single mom supporting two kids. She did a nice job, particularly moving rendition of "Amazing Grace." Big hit with the tourists. I overheard someone say what courage she must have. Yes, I thought. Undeniably. And yet it occurred to me that she's only doing what she has to, what she knows, to survive.

November 11

Nick's leg no better so took him to the hospital today. Doctor ordered an X-ray and a blood test. Said there was something wrong in the bone but he wasn't sure what. Wants to do another test next week, some kind of scan of the bone. I asked if it was absolutely necessary and the look he gave me made me feel unfit to be alive. Of course we'll do the test. That's about it for Claire's paycheck.

November 12

Had a sweet lovemaking with Claire. It's been awhile. Unseasonably warm night kept us from having to huddle under blankets. She has such a beautiful body, the swale of her belly like some flawless planet, a geography made all the more perfect by the pale thin scar half-hidden in her pubic hair where the doctors cut her open to deliver Nick. She told me once she had feared an ugly scar more than the surgery itself. She's still self-conscious, even though it's barely visible. She rarely lets me touch it, and I've stopped telling her it's as lovely as any of her natural landmarks. Lovelier, because it reminds me of her courage. She doesn't believe me.

Instead, I ask myself if I would have the same courage, given the opportunity. What would require it? Scars do not bother me. Nor am I especially frightened by the possibility of bodily injury. Some threat to my son? My wife? Undoubtedly. But for myself, only myself, what terrifies most is failure. It haunts my inner life, and I do whatever I can to avoid it. My act of courage, if it ever comes, will be to abandon ambition forever.

November 14

Finished Chapter Twelve, one more to go. Even at this late stage there are surprises. Jaime turned unexpectedly dour, revealing a side to himself that augurs darkly for the book. Suggests an ending I'd hoped to avoid. People are willing to consider suffering but only as a tonic. Redemption must prevail.

But this book will be a success, I swear it. By the end Jaime will reveal yet another layer, a deeper one. A well-spring of faith and abiding love. I know it's there. Even the hardest hearts will weep.

November 15

I came home today to find Claire yelling at Nick. He was standing beside the refrigerator, cowering and trying not to cry. Between them on the floor lay a mess of broken eggs. Claire lifted him roughly by the arms and moved him to the side. In a voice shaking with anger she ordered him to his room.

When he was gone, I asked what had happened. She gave me a bleak look, then knelt on the floor and buried her face in her hands.

"I hate this," she muttered. "I hate it, hate it, hate it."

"I'll get some more."

She looked up accusingly. "With what?"

"You don't have to take it out on Nick."

She started to reply, then her eyes filled with tears.

"Claire . . ."

She waved me away. "How does it get like this? Suddenly you see yourself doing something you never dreamed you could. That awful glimpse. The shame . . ."

"Talk to him. Tell him."

"I wish we had money."

"We will."

"I don't mean a lot. Some." Wearily, she got to her feet. "It's not his fault."

She left the kitchen, and I stared at the mess. Half a dozen broken eggs is not a pretty sight. My responsibility? Maybe so.

Taking the rag in hand, I cleaned the floor, then went and found that ad in the newspaper. The same woman answered the phone, same cordial, pleasant voice. As though she were the guardian of some secret of contentment and happiness. I made the appointment to give her my blood.

November 16

The monkey sits on our head, we sit on the monkey. I finish the book, and an hour later the doctor calls to say that Nickie has cancer. Cancer. What is the heart to do? Between exhilaration at completing the book and this sudden grief, my heart chooses the latter. It is my son. They want to cut off his leg.

November 20

Another battery of tests. Doctors now unsure whether to amputate or try to cure with radiation and drugs. We are nearly broke. The two-hundred dollars I'll have after tomorrow will stake us to another week, maybe two if we stretch it. Medical bills will just have to wait. By the time we get the second collection notice the book should be sold.

November 21

   The question of worthiness plagues me. Am I a good husband? A father? A writer? In moments of clarity I see fame as the culmination of fear, success another name for sacrifice. Ambition has a way of being unforgiving.

   The appointment was on Larkin St., in a fancy old apartment building on Russian Hill. Its entrance was framed by marble pillars and lined by enormous stone urns the color of sand. At the top of the stairs was a glass door with a polished brass casing and a single doorbell. I was buzzed inside by a uniformed guard who asked my business. I gave him my name, which he checked on a clipboard before pointing me to a door at the rear of the lobby. It opened onto an old-fashioned elevator with a hand-operated metal gate. There were eight floors to the building and I took the elevator to the top, where I stepped out into a carpet-lined hallway lit by a single, large chandelier. Opposite me was a door with the number I'd been given.

   A blue-suited man with a pleasant, generically handsome face let me in, addressing me by name without bothering to introduce himself. He was a head taller than me and at least that much wider across the shoulders. His handshake was just firm enough to enforce the already unmistakable impression of latent strength.

   He led me through a door into a second room many times larger than the first, full of furniture, sculptures and paintings. I recognized a Van Gogh, marvelling at the quality of the reproduction until I realized that it was probably the original. A brass head I had once seen in an art book lay casually propped on a table. Beside it was a richly upholstered couch and at the far end of the room a grand piano, its black top gleaming.

   The opulence was overwhelming, and it was some time before I ventured away from the door. Mindful of all the precious objects, I crossed to a picture window on the other side of the room. It was a relief to look out, like having a sip of plain water after a meal of sweets.

The view was breathtaking. To the west lay the city, to the north the bay, its water gray in the blunted afternoon light. I had the impression I was staring out from a gigantic eye, far from the poverty to which I was accustomed. It was a safe, antiseptic view, and for an instant the sun broke through the clouds, throwing a bright slit of light across the water. In that moment of beauty I forgot my sorrow, but then a door closed, breaking the reverie.

I turned, expecting to see the totem-like man who had ushered me in. Instead, it was a woman. She had a youngish look about her but moved with the deliberation of someone older. She wore a skirt and open-necked blouse, and her skin was either lightly tanned or else naturally dark. She introduced herself simply as Devora, and as soon as she spoke, I recognized the voice of the woman on the telephone.

We sat opposite each other on the sofa, and I casually remarked that it was a beautiful room, not at all what I'd expected for a medical interview. She replied that there was no reason for research to be conducted in austerity and went on to explain that the foundation she represented was small and personal enough to be attentive to such niceties.

"Those who work for us suffer few hardships," she said, then opened a folder on her lap and began with her questions.

Most pertained to my health but others concerned my family, marriage, even my financial situation. Some were quite personal, and initially I was reluctant to discuss them. Devora was an attractive woman, her nails carefully manicured, her hair meticulous. She wore several thin gold necklaces, which she had a habit of twirling through her fingers. It was a mannerism that, taken with her scrupulous beauty, called to mind a vanity that did not inspire my trust. In every other way, though, she seemed open and sincere, so that after awhile I found myself willing to confide in her. I spoke briefly of my troubled career as a writer, my aspirations and current hopes for success. I mentioned Claire's dissatisfaction with work and, after a moment's hesitation, told her of the tumor in Nickie's leg. She made a note on her paper, then closed the folder and rewarded me with a look of sympathy and understanding.

"The human body can be so fragile," she said. "I'm very sorry."

"The doctors talk of a cure."

"Of course."

"He's receiving radiation and drugs. We're hopeful."

"Certainly. And if the boy does not respond. What then?"

I was taken aback. "What kind of a question is that?"

"You must have considered it."

"It's none of your business."

"Forgive me."

A silence ensued, which she seemed in no hurry to break.

"They'll have to cut it off," I muttered. "Give him some sort of fake leg."

"A prosthesis."

I nodded.

"If it were possible for your son to receive a real leg, one of flesh and blood, would you consent?"

"I don't understand."

"A living limb. A transplant."

"The doctors have never mentioned that."

"The operation is rarely done," she said with authority. "The donor requirements are so strict as to virtually prohibit it "

"Then why do you ask?"

"The foundation is interested in the attitudes people have toward transplantation."

"It must be expensive."

"Forgetting the cost."

I gave her a look.

"Come now. You're a writer. A thinker. Take it as a philosophical question." She played with a necklace. "If a limb were available, if it could be grafted on, would you consent?"

.I sensed that some trap was being laid, but she did not seem the type. Still, I felt the need to consider carefully. I stood and walked to the window. The clouds now covered the whole of the city, bathing it in a marbled, celestial light.

"Yes," I said at length. "I'd consent. What father would not want his child whole?"

"It is a great gift."

"You have children?"

"One," she said without elaboration. She looked at her watch, then stood and smoothed her skirt. "You've been very patient."

She led me to a door opposite the one she had entered and motioned me inside. When I realized she was not going to follow, I stopped and asked about the money.

"You'll receive a check within the week."

I hesitated briefly before asking if there were some way to be paid sooner. She started to say one thing, then stopped herself.

"Of course. I'll take care of it. And again, many thanks for your cooperation."

She left, leaving me alone in this new room. It was small and windowless, unpleasantly lit by a fluorescent rectangle of over-head light. In the center was a narrow table, on either side of which was an armless plastic chair. In one corner was a sink and in another, a refrigerator. Black and white photographs graced the walls, highly magnified views of people's faces. I was studying the lobe of an ear when a man entered the room. He wore a white lab coat and looked uncannily like the man I had first met. He had me sit opposite him at the table, then opened a drawer and brought out a needle, syringe and tourniquet. After tying the tourniquet around my arm, he slid the needle swiftly into a vein, causing the barest whisper of pain, and drew off five or six tubes of blood. He finished almost as soon as he had started, releasing the tourniquet and pasting a small bandaid on top of the punc-ture wound. He marked the tubes with a pen, aligned them in a metal rack at the end of the table, then stood up with the rack in hand. He thanked me and pointed to a door, then turned and exited by another. Opening the one he had indicated, I found myself in the very first room I had entered.

I was disoriented, and stood for a moment wondering what to do. Just then, yet another door opened and the man in the blue suit who had first greeted me appeared. From his vest pocket he took out a plain white envelope, which he handed to me. I was embarrassed to look but felt foolish not to, and ended up turning my back and quickly checking the contents. Satisfied, I slid the envelope in my coat pocket, thanked him and left.

In the elevator I looked in the envelope again. Four fifty-dollar bills, as crisp as crackers. Easy money. It made me want to come back.

November 29

Tony is lukewarm on the book. He tries to be kind, says things like "it's idiosyncratic. Challenging." He wants more of a resolution, meaning, if not complete sunshine, at least a healthy glow of happiness at the end. "Does Jaime have to suffer so much?" he asks. I feel like telling him to ask Jaime, instead reply that suffering is the human condition, is only a small step on the larger road to enlightenment. I tell him this is a story about love and love involves sacrifice.

"We're just a breath away from paradise here," I hear myself saying. "Let the people judge. They've learned from their soap operas. They know how to pick a winner."

November 30

Got a letter from Devora and The Kingman Foundation today. Says if I'm interested in further work to give them a call. I'm not. The conversation yesterday with Tony has left me surprisingly upbeat about my chances with the book. I'm a writer. I'll wait.

December 6

Nick is brave as hell. He limps all the time, obviously in pain, but he hardly ever complains. Worst thing for him is not being able to go out with the guys after school. By then he's so exhausted he has to come home for a nap. Sleeps until dinner. His appetite's off, doctors say the treatments will do that. Claire's a wreck, seeing him like this. Like a part of herself has ceased to function properly. I'm not much better. We're barely eating, waking five, six times a night out of worry.

This thing's a family disease.

December 11

Met with Nick's doctors today. Grave men, but humane. Treatment not going as well as they'd hoped. Nick can't tolerate the doses they need to eradicate the tumor. All agreed to give it another couple of weeks. If no response, amputation.

I asked about a transplant. Difficult, they say, much harder than kidney or even heart. Cadavers don't work, donor has to be living and vital. Limbs remain viable for less than an hour after death.

"Obviously hard to find a living person willing to part with his leg," says one of the doctors.

"Prosthetics are getting better all the time," says another.

I ask about cost.

"A lot," says the doctor in charge.

"What? A hundred thousand?"

"More."

"Two?"

"After it's all over, probably half a million."

A daunting figure. I glance at Claire, who's staring at the floor, trying to contain herself. Anger rises in me, and then from nowhere an overwhelming sense of failure. Irrational as it is, I feel responsible.

December 13

The city is filled with the smoke from a brush fire a hundred miles to the east. Tiny white ashes float in the air, as though this were the day of judgment. People go methodically about their business without the slightest concern. I myself feel at the mercy of circumstances beyond my control, ironically the first breath of fresh air in months.

We are dead broke. It's a kind of freedom. Stark, but unencumbered by the swamp of egotism and pride. Now I have no choice but to get a job. I spread the want-ads on the floor, poised with my foot to stamp at random, when the phone rings. It's Devora.

"You received our letter?" she asks.

"Letter?" I'm about to hang up, when I remember.

"We like to call to be sure," she says smoothly.

"Nicholas," I reply, embarrassed at my forgetfulness. "He's been a preoccupation."

"I understand."

Do you, I want to say, angry suddenly at her wealth and good health. Instead, I glance down at the newsprint under my foot. An ad for a school of technical and creative writing, promising exciting and rewarding careers. The ultimate self-indictment.

I tell her I'll take the job.

December 23

It's a funny kind of work. I've been poked and prodded by three different doctors, scanned by at least twice that many machines, had tubes passed down my throat and up my ass, blood drawn, eyes and ears checked, exercised, rested . . . it goes on. Some of the tests are done in the Larkin St. apartment, but most in a private and fancy little clinic near Mission Bay. Everyone's nice as can be, making me feel a bit guilty. These tests would cost anyone else thousands, and here I am getting paid to do them. And paid handsomely. It's the easiest money I've ever earned.

As Devora has explained it, the foundation's work is in the area of clinical transplantation, and according to her, they've been highly successful. My job, after this initial phase, will be to provide certain materials, such as hair and skin, for grafting. My tissues have been matched to another man, who will receive them. Although the work will be intermittent, as long as I remain available my salary will continue. Raises, she promises, will be frequent and generous.

January 22

It's been nearly a month now, and I've yet to be called on. From time to time I find myself wondering what it will be . . . a small piece of skin, a tuft of hair? For the most part, though, I've been too busy to think about it.

We've moved into a beautiful new apartment at the tip of Grant Ave. Three bedrooms, big kitchen and a living room with a fireplace and a spectacular view of the bay. I spend hours just sitting in my armchair, beer in hand, luxuriating in the warmth of a well-heated room and the panorama of sky and water. We bought a television and VCR for Nickie to use while he's going through the exercises with his new leg. He's doing remarkably well considering the amputation was little more than a month ago. Stump's all healed, he's got his energy back, raring to go. Amazing how he bounces back.

No word yet on the book, and other than these entries I'm not writing. I'm making good money as it is. Why torture myself to be rejected?

January 31

I was called today for my first "assignment." A few tufts of hair from the back part of my scalp. They use an instrument that looks a little like an apple corer, but much smaller. Because my hair is so thick the missing spots are hardly visible. The whole thing lasted about an hour and now I am back home, sucking on a beer and watching the rain sweep across the city. It's a lovely sight, and I feel no need to improve on it.

Lately, I've been wondering about the man on the other end. Devora says that someday I'll meet him, though she seems in no particular hurry. I gather that he's quite a bit older and not in the best of health. Selfishly, I find myself hoping that, even in sickness, he survives a long time.

The part of my scalp where they took the hair is virtually healed. The scabs came off yesterday, which makes the itching much less. The rectangle of skin from my inner thigh, however, is another matter. They used something called a microtome, which supposedly takes off only the thinnest of layers, but it feels as if they branded me with an iron. The area is all red and hurts like hell to touch. I haven't been able to go out because my pants rub against it. No sex all this week.

February 13

Second week and skin graft still not healed. Somehow it got infected, which isn't supposed to happen. Now I'm on antibiotics and bedrest to air it out. The doctors couldn't be nicer, but I'm not used to being sick. Makes me cantankerous. To top it off Tony called with bad news. Because of disappointing sales of my first two books, they're not making an offer on the new one. Fine. Let them wither in the heat of my future fame and success.

February 20

Damn sore finally healed enough that Claire could touch me without my feeling she was sticking a knife in my leg. We made love gingerly, despite the weeks of pent-up desire. Afterwards, I found myself unconsciously fingering the scar on her belly. She didn't seem to mind, maybe because she was busy trying to arouse me again.

"This stays," she said.

"You bet."

"I mean it. It's one part I'll never let them take." Her face was hidden, and I couldn't tell if she was joking. The idea sent shivers down my spine.

February 24

I met Kingman Ho today, after whom the foundation is

named. A tall man with a face that was once probably handsome, he was looking out the big picture window in the living room when I arrived. Devora introduced us, and I held out a hand that he did not immediately take. Instead, he looked at me from behind his thick glasses with eyes that were impossible to read. I remembered gazing out over the city on my first visit, thinking it lovely though distant and dreamlike. The feeling I had as he looked at me was much the same but in reverse, as though I were a landscape of his own imagination. Either that or an article of clothing he was appraising.

It made me uncomfortable and I became conscious of my imperfections, the faint scar on my cheek from a boyhood accident, the part of my nose that was broken in a fall. For some reason I felt I should apologize, but instead mumbled some inane comment about the view. He looked at me quizzically, as if surprised that I was capable of speech, and turned to Devora, who whispered something in his ear. He nodded and managed to smile at me, then left the room. Devora adjusted one of the necklaces at her throat.

"He likes you," she said, an assessment that seemed beyond the realm of anyone's knowledge. I asked what made her say so.

"He has no choice," she replied. "Kingman is ill. You may have noticed."

"He seemed distant."

"Renal osteodystrophy," she said cryptically. "His bones are like egg shells."

"He's in pain?"

"Great pain," she said. "Seldom will you meet a braver man "

I thought of Nick, who more than once has humbled me with his courage.

"My son is brave."

She stared out the window, nodding ever so slightly. "They say that courage is contagious. How is the boy doing?"

"Well. He's already walking."

"The money is sufficient? There's been no interference with his care?"

"You've been more than generous."

She nodded again, this time turning to face me. "They say that that, too, is contagious."

She left the room before I had a chance to ask what she meant, and a moment later I followed, ushered out by the man in the blue suit.

At home tonight I looked up the disease in a book. Something having to do with kidney failure, the bones becoming wafer thin because all the calcium leaches out. Later on in bed, I found myself rubbing my flank, and Claire, sensing that something was troubling me, stilled me with her hand. Then she kissed where I had been rubbing, outlining the area with her tongue, as if to describe a future scar to match her own. An uncanny woman, choosing just the right moment to show her tenderness.

"I love you no matter who you are," she murmured, as she has so many times before. It makes all the difference.

February 27

Devora dropped by today, ostensibly to see the apartment and meet Claire. She wore a gay-looking dress with a scooped collar and the omnipresent gold chains at her throat. Claire was cordial but ill-at-ease, and I could tell from the beginning she was waiting for the visit to be over. At a certain point she excused herself to make tea, and Devora used the opportunity to inform me of some upcoming work. At the same time she handed me a "bonus" check of ten thousand dollars. I stared at it for a moment, then folded it and put it away.

"Please don't mention this to Claire," I said, sensing it was unnecessary to ask. "It's always been hard for her to accept good fortune. I'll tell her later."

"Be politic when you do," said Devora. "I don't want her to fear me more than she does."

"What she fears is the sudden wealth."

"Perhaps." She was pensive. "And you?"

"I fear that it will end."

March 8

A week now since they took the kidney. Except for some pain when I turn or move fast, I don't even notice that it's gone. The initial shock of being asked to part with it has passed. So, too, the surprise that the recipient is Kingman Ho himself. Wealth makes its own rules. I look at it like this: if Nickie or Claire needed a kidney in order to live, would I offer one of mine? Without a second thought. So isn't what I'm giving them now nearly the same? A decent place to live, food when they're hungry, heat, clothing. By donating my kidney to Ho, I'm simply giving my family a life they deserve.

March 21

Attended a small party at the Larkin St. apartment this evening. After considerable persuasion Claire agreed to come, and Nick joined us. We were met by the nameless man in the blue suit, who took our coats and ushered us into the living room. Devora stood beside the piano, drink in hand, talking to a woman who might well have been her twin. Kingman Ho was nearby, surrounded by a clump of judicious looking, well-tailored men. Several couples stood at the window, taking in the magnificent view, and beyond them, warming themselves by the fireplace, two of the doctors who had examined me. A servant in a starched black dress brought us drinks, and a few minutes later a girl served us hors d'oeuvres from a silver tray. She couldn't have been more than a year or two older than Nick, though her manners were those of an adult well-trained in service. She held out the tray to Nickie, who didn't know quite what to do. He looked to me for help, while the girl, in complete possession of herself, urged him to take one of her tidbits. I nodded my approval, then took one myself, a bit of cracker heaped generously with caviar. It was delicious, and I had another.

At length Devora came over with Kingman, clinging un-
ashamedly to him as if he were some prize catch. I did not immediately grasp the significance of this. Admittedly, the man looked
fitter than before, his color better, his attention crisper, but his
stolid manner seemed a world away from Devora's youthfulness
and vigor. She was a good twenty, even thirty years his junior, yet
here she was nuzzling his neck like some restless colt. It occurred
to me she might be a daughter, yet her attentions seemed anything but filial.

Kingman greeted me with more warmth than when we had
first met. He held my hand longer than was necessary, using the
opportunity to once again appraise me. This time I returned his
scrutiny, and after a moment he smiled, releasing me with a muttered word of appreciation. He introduced himself to Claire,
gracefully slipping her hand through his arm and steering her
away.

"He seems to have recovered his health," I said drily.

"Remarkably," replied Devora, looking after him. "He's a new
man."

"Perhaps I should be flattered.'"

She considered this, then took a step closer. She was a little
drunk. "For the first time in years he performs like a man." She
touched a necklace, smiling to herself. "I had all but forgotten.
Imagine. Now I am called on to be a woman again. Who would
have thought?"

"I'm happy for you," I said, but in truth I was not. It seemed
wrong that Ho, already so much older than she, was performing
with a body not wholly his. More than that, it seemed improper,
as though I were being used in some strange and undignified way
as a sex surrogate. This I had never agreed to, and I was about to
say something when Devora's look-alike interrupted us. She introduced herself, and I casually asked if the two of them were
twins.

"You flatter me," said Devora.

"My mother knows the secret of youth," said the woman. She

brushed a piece of stray hair from Devora's cheek and whispered something in her ear. Devora nodded and the woman, excusing herself, left.

"Mother?" I said. "To her? She can't be less than thirty."

"A beautiful girl," said Devora proudly.

"How old are you?"

She smiled coyly, touching one of her necklaces. Just then a piece of wood caught fire, momentarily brightening the room. It cast a sudden light on her throat, revealing a thin white scar at the base of her neck. I stared at it, then her eyes. They were laughing at me.

"The others are well-hidden," she said.

"I'm embarrassed."

"Don't be." She lifted a glass of wine from a passing tray, holding it aloft as if in toast. "What greater act of creation than to create ourselves?"

Later that evening, watching the fog slip through the gate, I happened to catch Nick out of the corner of an eye. He was sitting on the floor at the far end of the room, partially obscured by one of the piano legs. Kneeling next to him was the serving girl. At first I thought they were playing some game, so enrapt were they, but after edging a little closer, I saw they were doing something different entirely. Nick had his pant leg rolled up, and the girl was fingering his prosthesis. Inch by inch she was creeping up the leg, circling it one moment, stroking it the next, coddling it as though she were unearthing some priceless relic. Nick was utterly entranced, as mesmerized by the girl's attention as she was by his false limb. When she came to the edge of his pant leg, she'd stop and glance up, waiting for him to roll the pants up further. Little by little the entire limb was becoming exposed. By the look on his face Nick seemed actually to be feeling the girl's touch, as though the intensity of her exploration were awakening some hitherto slumbering receptors in his phantom limb. There was a charge I could feel from across the room. I was torn about what to do, feeling on the one hand that it was my responsibility as a father to intervene and on the other, that to interrupt now might only reinforce the stigma of Nickie's handicap. The choice was made moot when one of the adult servants found the girl and with angry words pulled her from the room. The spell broken, Nickie became suddenly self-conscious, fumbling abashedly with his pant leg. I rushed over and helped him to his feet, saying nothing of what I had seen. I suggested it was time to leave, and, after looking quickly around the room, presumably for the girl, Nick agreed. I had an arm on his shoulder but he shrugged me off, preferring to make his exit alone.

He fell asleep in the car on the way home, but a parent can never be sure. I decided to hold off telling Claire of the incident, and to pass the time I asked her opinion of Kingman Ho. They had spent nearly an hour together.

"I think there's something terribly wrong with him," she said. "We weren't together for ten minutes before I wanted to comfort him. A complete stranger. It's not what I expected."

"Suffering has a certain allure. Ho's been ill with one thing or another for years."

"When he speaks of himself, it's as though he were someone else. Once he said something, I don't remember what, and I found myself thinking, this is a man who lives in a mirror. A brittle, distant mirror."

"He's arrogant. And rich. I think he makes a point of staying aloof."

"He told me he holds himself in contempt. I asked him why and he said for lacking the strength to die."

"He's posing, Claire. It's cocktail party conversation."

"He scares me," she said, shivering against the cold and pulling Nick into her. "I wish we didn't depend on him."

"You have it backwards," I told her, angry that she had been affected this way. "I'm the one who holds the aces. Kingman Ho depends on me."

May 3

Last month it was the small bones in my ear. A week later, my right eye. It's amazing how quick I adapt. Unless someone whispers to my left, I hear almost as well as before. And except for a certain flatness of vision, which becomes less noticeable each day, my eyesight is unchanged.

I run into Ho from time to time. He is polite, even cordial, and ironically I'm now the one who's keeping a distance. There's little I have to say to him, and what I do usually comes out rudely. The fact is I don't like him. He takes and takes like a spoiled child, and what does he give in return? Money. It's a cold reward.

Nevertheless, when we meet, I look for signs in him of recognition. I often find myself staring at his right eye, the brown one stippled with green, the one that is mine. It looks stony in his face, callous, yet every so often it takes on a gleam too familiar to ignore. I know your motives, it seems to say. You cannot lie.

Sometimes I want to claw the eye from his face.

May 5

Tony called . . . another rejection. I told him I don't care. For the first time that I remember I feel liberated from the yoke of the marketplace.

May 17

There is something erotic to all this. It embarrasses me to say so because it sounds perverse. Yet each time they take part of my body, my sexuality becomes heightened. The toes were taken a week and a half ago, and since then I've been in a state of constant erection, having wet dreams nearly every night. Claire, always before my sexual match, has been eclipsed by this newfound desire. It's as if my unconscious, fearful of its survival, has panicked, triggering a surge of sexuality in the hopes of perpetuating my genetic stock before I suffer extinction.

At times I have the feeling I am approaching a new and primitive state, one of explosive creativity and gratification. The

compulsion for language and abstract thought has become remote, making me wonder why I ever bothered writing at all. In
comparison to the language of the body, words say so little.

Claire, who knows me perhaps better than I know myself,
thinks I'm a little mad.

May 23

They want my arm. My right arm. Shoulder to fingertip. I'm
afraid.

May 31

This past week has felt like a year. The fear of apprehension
is with me constantly. The blue-suited bodyguard will appear,
blandly crushing me in his arms and taking me back. Or Devora
will arrive, bearing some new manner of persuasion. A subtle
change of posture, a lilt in her voice, the veiled promise of some
favor impossible to refuse. Or Kingman himself, man of few
words, instigator of my flight. Armless now, with no finger to pull
the trigger, no hand to make me dance to his insane command.
He will come to beg for my limb.

Let him. Let him feel my contempt at his wealth and power.
He is not a man. No man would do to me what he has done.

More than anything, I fear my own uncertainty. I could tell
them I'm through and put a stop to this thing once and for all. Or
else give them the arm and be done with it. Why run?

Wealth and success are not easy to dismiss. What if Kingman
dies? Kingman the Brute, the Cruel. My patron. What then?

June 3

The wind howls in the canyons, scouring the earth with sand.
The heat of the desert sun is unbelievable. I hide in my motel
room and wait. I'm convinced they know where I am. Why don't
they come?

*   *   *

June 5

One's self-importance diminishes greatly out here. The desert is too big, too raw and exposed to suffer pride and deceit. I see that my hatred for Ho is little more than the mirage of my own inadequacy. I cannot despise him for wanting my arm anymore than I can despise my son for wanting a new leg. It's man's nature to fight disintegration and decay.

But more, I begin to see that Kingman Ho and I are linked. Each layer of skin, each organ that I give weds him more firmly to me. Ho is my creation. Running from him is tantamount to running from myself.

June 29

Absence is a stronger state than presence. It derives shape from the imagination, from loss and need. The arm has been gone for weeks, but when I close my eyes it is still there. I feel sensations in thin air, pain, heat, motion. I hold a pencil, a cup of coffee in a phantom world, stroke Claire's back and feel the texture of her skin with a hand that can't be seen. But something exists, I know it, something that could not be severed from the tracts of memory.

I imagine the arm hanging from Kingman's side, attached to his nerves and muscles, moving to his command but all the while maintaining a deeper program, untempered by conscious thought. I picture the hand accenting the air with my mannerisms, writing in my script, stroking Devora with my touch. The limb is a ghost, and I, the ghost writer. As I serve Kingman, he serves me.

July 2

We have more money now than we know what to do with. Claire has quit her job, and Nick has private tutors to help him make up the time he's lost. I read rather than write, or else sit in the armchair with a beer and watch the bay change colors. I don't feel lazy. My job is to heal.

July 15

It's surprising how fast I recover from these operations. Just a few days ago they took a piece of bone from my pelvis, and already I'm able to move around quite well. Except for the skin graft months ago, I've had no problems whatever. I can't say the same for Kingman. Even though our tissues are matched, he still seems to struggle through almost every procedure. His age must have something to do with it, and Devora says the drugs he takes to keep from rejecting my tissue get in the way of his healing. It's hard to see anyone suffer as he does. I pity him and sometimes wonder why he persists. Does he truly fear death, or is there some other reason that he prolongs his life? Perhaps immortality is a motive in itself.

July 18

Woke up from a dead sleep last night wondering, of all things, what Kingman had for dinner. Not simply the menu but how he had eaten, and with whom. Was it a lively, high-spirited meal or tiresomely dull; a pleasure or, in his old age, a chore? Did he eat alone or with company? In suit and tie or more casually dressed? What did he say? What did he think and not say?

It took me an hour to get back to sleep, and in the morning I needed two cups of coffee to wake up. As I poured the second, I tried to remember if I'd ever seen Kingman drink coffee. Black or with cream? One cup or two?

July 21

Why haven't they called? It's been nearly a week without a word. Something bad has happened, I know it. Two things come frightfully to mind. Kingman has finally gotten too sick to need me. Bad enough, but the other is worse.

They've found a new donor.

July 24

Finally. Early this morning, pitch black outside, the phone

rang. It triggered a dream and I reached out to Claire with my phantom limb. She murmured something and nestled into my empty socket. I picked up the receiver.

His voice was urgent, lacking its familiar polish and restraint. He demanded to see me immediately, insisting that I meet him at his apartment. I agreed, but when I asked what was the matter, the phone was already dead.

Outside, the fog had settled to ground-level, as thick as if it had sprung from the earth itself. Kingman's building was all but invisible from the street, the tall Greek columns seemingly anchored to clouds. A night clerk let me in, saying that Mr. Ho was expecting me. I wiped the moisture from my face and hair and entered the elevator. At the eighth floor I started to exit when Kingman suddenly appeared, shoving me back inside. He pulled the gate shut, hit the down button, then stopped the elevator between floors.

"The records," he said, facing me with wild, bloodshot eyes. "Where are the records?"

I searched my mind for some previous mention of records. Something to orient me. But he did not wait for a reply.

"I need to know what they're doing. All of them. Earnest faces, yes, but none as honest as they pretend. I've tried to get messages out. It's some game, isn't it? Some imposter's ploy . . ."

"Game? I don't understand."

"Why are they giving me four pills at night and only three in the morning? Tell me that, if you can."

"Four? Three?"

"It's a charade, isn't it? An imitation." He grinned, as though pleased with himself, but the look was quickly gone. "It moves on channels beyond what the others can detect. It's lost to them, but not to us. Tell me, who are the higher authorities? Who pulls the strings?

"I'm asking for your help," he said, more urgently now. "Tell me what to do. I hear them talk. Even behind my back, it's obvious what they're saying. But I will not be discouraged."

"They couldn't do this to an ordinary man. I see it, and I am above it. When I will it to stop, it will stop. Do you understand? It's my duty."

His voice was high-pitched, his manner desperate. He paced frantically, while taking care, it seemed, not to touch me. All at once he stopped.

"Can you smell the decay? Even a strong person can't hold out forever. I need answers. Help me."

The man was clearly out of his mind, and I worried that the tiny space we were in was making him worse. I inched over to the elevator's control panel, eyeing the switch that would set us in motion, but as soon as I got close, he blocked my way. With a menacing look he leaned against the panel, bracing himself with both feet planted firmly on the floor. He placed his palms together in an attitude either of prayer or warning and shut his eyes.

For the first time I got a good look at him. His hair was disheveled, his face mottled and red. His skin was marked by scores of tiny capillaries, many of which had burst. At one side of his neck, peeking above his shirt collar, was the edge of a recent skin graft. It was swollen and purple, with a crust that oozed yellowish liquid. I felt an urge to run, which was impossible, but also to comfort him. He seemed in furious pain, and had now put himself in a position of no escape. But when I stepped forward in an effort to help him, he opened his eyes and growled at me. I tried some words to calm him, but he only laughed, accusing me of trying to control him with my voice.

"I see what you're thinking," he said. "Trying to trick me with your deep tones. Don't you see that I'm your reflection? This is no joke."

He started humming to himself, an hysterical tune of his own making. Suddenly, the elevator began to move. His head darted frantically from side to side, and he slapped at the control. To no avail. Inexorably the car ascended, and at the eighth floor the blue-suited man was there to pull back the gate. Beside him, in slippers and bathrobe, stood Devora. The sight of her seemed to take something out of Kingman, who, having backed into a corner, let out a shuddering sigh and collapsed against the elevator wall.

We carried him into the apartment, and twenty minutes later Devora returned to tell me everything was all right.

"I must apologize for my husband's behavior." She offered me a drink, which I readily accepted. "Some of these drugs have such terrible effects."

"I don't know which of us was more scared."

"Him, I imagine." She took her drink to the window. "He's not himself these days."

"I'm not surprised."

She stiffened. "The irony does not escape me. But no, he's not." She sighed. "I suppose it's a wonder that things don't change any faster than they do."

I had no reply and stared with her out the window, the reflection of our faces seeming to float in the fog.

"Have you ever written a book, then thrown it out? Destroyed it because it wasn't what you knew you could create, what you wanted to?"

"A book changes in the writing," I told her. "And then later, after. It could always become something else, something to cherish."

"Do you fall in love with what you write?"

"I suppose. Of a kind. It's always a stormy affair."

"But when things go bad, when they go astray, you know what to do."

I shrugged, and then all at once I understood what she was asking. "Someday Kingman will die," I told her. "Then you'll find out for yourself."

"I know how I'll act," she said quietly, as if she'd already planned it out. She seemed grateful to be able to tell me. "Is that shameful?"

"It's too early in the morning for shame."

"Yes." She touched a necklace and turned. "Do you find me attractive?"

I worked on my drink. She watched me and waited.

"You know the answer," I said at length. "You wouldn't have asked if you didn't."

"Vanity is such a scourge," she said with a self-deprecating little laugh.

I examined myself, my missing arm, toes and the rest.

"Isn't it."

July 28

Tonight, after I read him a bedtime story, Nick grabbed onto my arm and wouldn't let go. After a few minutes I asked him to stop, but he held on tighter.

"Nickie, it's bedtime."

"You have to stay," he said.

"I won't let you go."

"Three minutes," I said, relenting. "And then you sleep."

"You count."

The minutes passed, and when the time was up, Nickie still wouldn't let go.

"You have to leave your hand with me," he said.

"I've only got one left," I answered jokingly, touched by his possessiveness.

"Promise you won't take it away."

"I'm right next door, Nickie. I'm not going anywhere."

"Promise."

"I'm your father," I said. "You can't lose me." Gently, I pulled my arm away. "I love you, Nickie. I promise."

July 30

Claire and I lie naked in bed, her fingers working my back. One vertebra at a time, outlining each bone and muscle. I savor her touch, though I can't help wondering if she is taking inventory. When she reaches the nub at the bottom of my spine, the little upturning before it dives between the buttocks, she stops. I make sounds to indicate that she should continue, but she is still. All at once she starts to talk.

"When I was a kid, there was a boy. Joe something. He was older than me, with big buck teeth. Always popping his gum and showing his teeth. He used to get me in corners and rub up against me. Front to back, front to front if I didn't turn around fast enough. It was awful."

"You just remembered?"

"Joe something." Absently she touches me where she'd left off. "He had a tail."

"What?"

"A little tail. I didn't find out until later, after he had an operation to get rid of it. I was so happy when I heard."

"Why were you happy?"

"It seemed fair. Making me suffer like that, he should suffer too. I felt better just knowing that he'd suffered."

"Is this some message, Claire? A parable?"

"It's true."

"What's true?"

She traces the scar on my flank, taking her time. "Would it have been different if Nickie had not lost his leg? I'd still be working, you still troubled and angry. Things balance out. There's a funny kind of logic to all this."

"We have money."

"I'm happy for that. But something else."

"I'm dense tonight, Claire. What's on your mind?"

"I don't know." She touches the nub at the bottom of my spine, rubbing it as if to conjure the proper explanation. "It has to do with self-respect. Knowing the measure of things. The limits.

"You can stop whenever you want, Matt. This is not for money, it's not for me or Nickie. You must know that."

"I have inklings."

"Will you stop?"

"When I'm done. Yes. I promise."

August 8

My face is bandaged so that only my mouth and nostrils are in contact with the air. Sometimes I think I am being reduced to the point that nothing will remain of me but holes. Mercifully, I am heavily drugged.

This last operation was a tough one, and it was complicated by an infection. I write this by dictaphone, which someone, Claire probably, has left by the pillow. Kingman developed a sudden, overwhelming necrosis of his face, a result of one of the drugs he's on. The skin from forehead to chin, ear to ear sloughed off en masse. I was called in an emergency, and when I saw how he looked, the pain and fear in his eyes, I knew I would not refuse. So they brought me in and took my own face.

I am glad my eye is covered, because there are things I'd just as soon not see. Claire's look of woe, Nick's accusation and fear. I hear it well enough in their voices.

Tony called today, and while someone held the phone, he jabbered on excitedly about an offer from one of the big houses. Not much money, but an option clause that promises a lot if I deliver a second book within a year. So much has happened these last months that I had to ask him the name of the book they want to buy. He laughed and told me, then asked if I thought I could write another so soon. It was my turn to laugh, a feeble sound that barely escaped my lips.

"It's nearly done."

"The diary?" he asked. I must have mentioned it to him in a distant past. "You see it as a book?"

"Not that. The man. It's creation itself. Imagine, after all these years. You pray for success, you search in vain for the door, only to realize you've already walked through."

Someone is holding my hand. Claire, I think, though it might be Devora. Heavy sedation makes my senses less than keen.

Kingman has had a stroke. A massive one, and now his brain

is dead. The news has the recurring and obsessive feel of a dream, yet all the substance and plausibility of reality.

His brain is dead.

A work of art must breathe life.

There seems only one thing left to do.